About Last Knight After the party

By

Terrell Perry

All rights reserved. This book or any portion thereof may not be reproduced or used in any manner whatsoever without the express written permission of the publisher except for the use of brief quotations in a book review.

Printed in the United States of America

First Printing, 2017

ISBN #978-1-387-26448-3

Lulu Press, Inc.

627 Davis Drive, Suite 300, Morrisville, NC 27560

EPISODE 1

"RAVEN'S NIGHT OUT"

How did we end up like this? How did it come to this? Who would ever imagine staring down the barrel of a gun that's in the hands of their best friend? Now I know what you're thinking, "Why is your best friend pointing a gun at you?" Well, I guess I should start from the beginning.

For as long as I can remember I've lived a pretty boring life. I'm nothing like other twenty-five-year-old females. I don't go to clubs; I'm not a selfie queen, twerk video making, reality TV watching kind a girl. I usually spend my weekends at home curled up with a good book and a nice glass of Moscato. However, on this particular night, I had my five foot five, petite frame stretched out on the couch. I was completely lost in the pages of a romance novel about a forbidden love. I was just getting to the good part, where they are finally about to make love, when I hear the sound of someone struggling to get in the door. It could only be one person since I'm single, an only child, and my parents died years ago in an unfortunate accident while on vacation, but that is a story for another day.

Anyway, struggling to get into my apartment was my best friend Evelyn Jones, but she goes by Eve. Even though she was dressed down by her standards, she was looking stunning as usual. She had on a chocolate brown motorcycle jacket with a white V-neck shirt under it showing off way too much cleavage for my taste, these dark blue jeans that were stressed throughout and some bad ass brown leather knee high boots with the red bottoms. The heel on them made her look like a runway model. She wore her black hair in a cute little pixie cut that complimented the soft features of her oval shaped face. Her complexion was the color of a warm cup of caramel macchiato, with a body like a video vixen which she wasn't afraid to flaunt.

Eve stood in front of the couch where I was lying and dropped her shopping bags. I tried to hide behind my book because I knew what was coming next. "Come on girl, get that ass up! You're not about to spend another Friday night in the house reading" yelled Eve. I could hear a little attitude in her voice, but I just continued hiding my face behind my book as I proceeded to tell her I wasn't interested in going to some night club. Eve just smiled as she replied, "Good, because we aren't going to a club. My boyfriend is having a private get together and asked me to bring a friend, soooooo lets go bitch!" Now I have no reason not to go besides the fact I just don't want to go, so I just let out a sigh as I cover my face with my book.

Eve walked over to the couch, snatched the book off my face and said to me, "All you do is read these big ass books!" She was more aggravated than upset. I looked at her with my puppy dog face and said, "But I love my big ass books!" Eve was upset now. I could see it in her eyes and what she said next sealed my fate. Eve crossed her arms, and then said, "So how you plan on meeting a man if you're always in the house? What do you think he's gonna do just magically pop out one of these books?" Stunned, I was utterly speechless. She was right; I'll never meet someone if I'm always in the house. I sat there contemplating if I should go or not, as Eve stood there eager in her silence. We both knew the first person to respond lost. After a brief moment of silence, I gave in. "Fine I'll go this once", I said. You should have seen the excitement and joy on her face.

Eve grabbed me by the hand, snatching me up from the couch, almost knocking my glasses off my face. She made me grab some of her shopping bags as she snatched up the rest of them, "We are about to have so much fun" said Eve as she dragged me to my bedroom.

Forcing me to sit on the bed, Eve went through the shopping bags filled with expensive designer clothes. "I knew you wouldn't have anything to wear so I took the liberty of picking you up a couple of outfits", Eve muttered as she held different outfits up against my body. I looked at her like, "You know I'm not wearing that right". She had me trying on clothes like I was getting ready to attend the Hip Hop music awards. The dresses she picked out were too short, or the whole back was out, or the front was cut so low that it exposed all my lady parts. I was feeling so embarrassed just trying them on, there was no way in this world I would wear any of them out in public. After an hour of us disagreeing on almost every outfit, we finally agreed on what I was wearing. We decided on a nice pair of dark blue jeans that hugged me just right showing off all my curves. The top was a red, sparkling halter top that was completely backless and to finish off my outfit I had to wear them bad ass brown leather boots with the red bottoms. I wore my long jet-black hair in a ponytail. I even agreed to let Eve do my make-up. When she was done I knew she was pleased, she was smiling from ear to ear. She turned towards the mirror and said, "You are beat to the gods honey"

Eve was right, I did look good. She did my make-up giving me a more natural look that complimented my chestnut brown eyes and contours in my high cheek bones. She even had my eyebrows on fleek, and I don't even know what that means, I just know that's how Eve described them. I stood in front of the mirror admiring myself while Eve finished getting dressed. I was doing my little, "I think I'm cute dance" as I stood in the mirror. "You ready to go?" Eve stammered as she caught me dancing in the mirror. I immediately stopped dancing, trying to act like I was cleaning off the mirror.

"Girl don't even try it, I saw you! You think you cute?" Eve laughed, as she started to do her own little two step. Eve had on a little black dress that was too short and showing too much cleavage for my taste . As we both stood in the mirror making sure our makeup was right and hair was on point before stepping out I thought to myself, "This might be a fun night".

The party we were going to was located in Oakwood, a rich part of the city. I'm talking gated community style. There was even a guard that sat at the gate like Saint Peter. He almost didn't allow us access until Eve told him she was a guest of Jag. Oh yeah, Jag is Eve's new boo, and in her own words, "Girl I think I hit the jackpot". She never told me what he did for a living but what I do know is he has money. He is the one who has been sponsoring Eve's most recent shopping sprees and this brand new black Mercedes Benz coupe were riding in.

Eve and Jag have only been dating for a few months but she swears they're in love. Now that I think about it, this will be my first time meeting this Jag character. Anyway, once the guard heard his name he immediately lets us pass apologizing for the delay. I looked at her and said, "Who is this guy and why is he so important?" Smiling Eve replied, "My baby is the man around here." That still didn't tell me anything, but I just left it alone. We made our way through the gates into neighborhood and all its luxurious glory.

As we drove towards our destination, the inside of the houses were illuminating against the evening sky making it easy to see inside the homes. Giving us just a glimpse of the expensive furniture, and large televisions mounted on the walls like framed artwork.

Eve tapped me on the shoulder to get my attention. When I looked in her direction she was pointing ahead of us toward a home on top of a hill, "That's where we're heading", she said eagerly. The house was the largest home in the neighborhood. It sat on a hill at the end of a cul-de-sac, beckoning like a lighthouse at the edge of the sea. After another fifteen minutes of driving, we finally arrived at our destination. The valet opened the door for us and helped us out the car. The young man gave Eve a ticket, hopped in the car and drove away.

Eve grabbed me by the arm, hugging it tighly as we walked towards the entrance. "This is going to some much fun", said Eve. You could hear the joy and excitement in her voice. "Is this his house?" I asked curiously. "Girl yes! This is the first time he has invited me here" Eve replied, giggly like a little school girl. I stared at her with the most confused look on my face. "What do you mean this is the first time he's invited you over here? Haven't you two been dating for months?" But before she could answer we were standing at the front door of the house. She knocked twice and the door opened.

A large, brown skinned black man was looking down at us. He had to be at least 6'9" and like 350 lbs. of solid muscle. He looked like he was bred to knock people out. He had on what looked like combat gear; black pants, black boots and a black t-shirt that was clearly one size too small. I guess he thought it made him look more intimidating than he already did. He had no facial hair and a low haircut, a clear sign he must be ex-military. He stood there in the doorway for a moment causing an awkward silence. Finally, he said, "Ms. Jones, he has been expecting you. Who is this?" "Oh, this is my friend Raven, he knows I'm bringing her.", said Eve nervously. The large door man looked at me with those beady little eyes before allowing us entry. "Thank you," replied Eve with a hint of relief in her voice. As we entered the house I grabbed Eve by the arm, pulling her close so the giant doorman couldn't hear me, "bitch I thought you said he knew

I was coming!" I whispered. Trying to hold in her laugh, Eve said, "I might have told you a tiny lie, but look at this party! I couldn't let you miss this"

I really wasn't mad, I mean, this place was nice. The door we came in wasn't the front door but an entrance to the back of the house which led to the backyard. It looked like a scene right out of a movie. The backyard was half the size of a football field and filled with a nice number of well-dressed men and women. There were white Christmas tree lights running along the edge of the entire yard creating a border of soft light which produced a relaxing ambience. There were waiters walking around carrying golden trays of wine glasses with what I can only imagine to be some hard to pronounce fancy wine, and exotic looking hors d'oeuvres that I probably won't be trying. In the very back of the yard was a DJ playing the latest Hip Hop music that everyone was vibing to. Even Eve was doing her little dance as we watched the scene play out in front of us.

As we stood at the foot of the yard, a well dress man looked in our direction. He said something to the group he was conversing with, and then started to make his way towards us. "Oh my god here he comes!" said Eve. He made his way through the crowd of party goers as some greeted him, while others tried to get him to stop talk but he only had eyes for Eve. Jag was draped in an all-black, tailor made designer suit, with a starched, white button-down shirt and a red silk tie. He skin was a lighter shade of brown than Eve and his head was cleanly shaven. Topping off the look was a thin mustache and triangle shaped goatee. When Jag finally reached us, he was taller than I expected, not as tall as the "too tight" t-shirt wearing doorman, probably like 6'1. He walked up to Eve pulled her close and immediately started kissing her, talk about awkward. It felt like they were kissing for an eternity. I was just about to walk away when Eve slowly pulled away from Jag, "Honey this is my best friend Raven I was telling you about", said Eve as she stared into his eyes. He looks over to me and extends his hand, "So you're the Raven I've heard so much about. It's a pleasure to finally meet you" I shook his hand and it was soft like he has never done a hard day of work in his life; yet, it was also cold, like creepy cold. Maybe it was from holding his drink so I didn't make a big deal about it.

"I know you ladies just got here but would you mind if I stole Eve from you for a moment?" asked Jag never taking his eyes off Eve. "Sure, don't mind me, I'll be fine" I said hesitantly. "Are you sure?" Eve replied, trying to sound concerned. I tried to give her the, "bitch you better not leave me" look but she was too wrapped up in Jag to notice.

"Girl you're the best, I'll be back soon. Go mingle!" said Eve as Jag led her by the hand into the house, and just like that I was alone. I decided if I'm going to mingle I'm going to need a drink to calm my nerves. I looked into the sea of people scanning for one of those waiters carrying them fancy trays of champagne glasses. The closest waitress was to my far left so I had to go get her. She was dressed in what looked like a black one-piece swimsuit with these black fishnet stockings, an apron around her waist and black boots. I flagged her down, she stopped and handed me a drink before rushing off to finish her rounds.

So, I'm standing there enjoying the ambience of this party, sipping my champagne when the first man approaches me. After his failed attempt to get me to leave this party with him, I politely declined his invitations. Suddenly a steady stream of men started coming up to me telling me how beautiful I was and asking if I were a model. I don't like being rude so I entertained their conversations. All these guys could talk about was themselves; what type of company they owned, where they lived, and where they like to go for vacation. I was starting to get annoyed, declining one after another of these sorry attempts to get me to go home with them, so I was ready to go. This was fun but definitely not my scene. I started to head to towards the entrance when suddenly I saw him.

He entered the room with a confidence that demanded the room's attention, yet nobody seemed to notice he enter the party, as if he was standing in the shadows. Without my glasses, I couldn't get a good look from this distance, but what I could tell he was average height, with an athletic build. Like Jag, he wore an all-black tailor-made suit but that is where the similarities ended. The mysterious man accented his suit with a black button up shirt, no tie and had the first two buttons undone giving a glimpse of his muscular chest underneath. He stood in the entrance where Eve and I stood when we came in. He searched the crowd with his eyes like a predator tracking his prey. I couldn't make out the features of his face without my glasses, but something was drawing me to this man. I stood watching him as he continued looking through the crowd and then it happened. Our eyes made contact! For a moment, everything stilled. I felt him looking into my soul; I instantly blushed as I looked away. I felt the heat in my cheeks so I knew my light skinned self was bright red in the face. I didn't know what to do so out of habit I grabbed the end of my ponytail and twirled it with my finger, smiling at the thought of this mysterious man looking at me.

In the time, it took me to look away and look back in his direction he was gone; I'm talking about instantly disappeared. The one guy I wanted to come and talk to me has vanished into thin air. "Ugh, now I'm really ready to go!" I thought to myself as I started walking towards the exit. "Excuse me," said a deep voice from behind me. I whipped around so quick that I dropped my drink. "Oh, I'm so sorry, I didn't mean to frighten you" He replied. It was him, the guy who looked into my soul! He was standing inches from me and I could see his features clearly now. He was the color of expensive dark chocolate with a nicely groomed 5 o'clock shadow. His black hair was cut low with a mean 360 wave pattern. His skin was flawless, not a single blemish. He was still trying to clean up the spilled drink as I stood there admiring him.

"Let me get you another drink." he apologized as he signaled a waitress over to bring another drink. He handed me the glass of champagne and apologized once more.

"My name is Alexander, but you can call me Alex", he smiled. He had dimples with the prettiest smile! Oh, my goodness, can he get anymore cuter!?

"Hello Alex. My name is Raven, pleased to meet you", I replied trying not to blush. He reached out to shake my hand so I did the same. "The pleasure is all mine" he replied. His hands were strong, nothing like the hands of the other men I' met tonight. These were hands of a man who knew what a day of manual labor was about, yet he had a gentle touch.

"This doesn't seem like your kind of scene" he said

"Is it that obvious?"

He makes the hand gesture for "just a little" and chuckles.

"I'm here with my best friend. She is the one who dragged me out tonight"

"Well, I'm glad she made you come. You're a breath of fresh air compared to these superficial women in here."

"How do you know I'm not superficial?"

"Let's just say I'm an excellent judge of character"

"Is that right? So, what would I be doing if I wasn't here tonight?"

He looked at me as he started to rub his chin. I could tell by looking into his dark brown eyes that he was conjuring up his answer in his mind.

"Ok, I got it"

"Let's hear it", I said eager to hear his answer.

"If you weren't here tonight, you would be at home lounging around reading a good book. You look like a romance novel type, but you also like a good adventure. Am I close?"

"Did he just read me like book?" I thought to myself. "Wow that's pretty impressive, only it wasn't a romance novel, it was an adventure novel" I answered trying not to sound into him.

"The novel had everything in it, excitement, romance, mystery all the things my life is currently missing"

"Be careful what you wish for, you just might get it"

"I know, but sometimes a girl needs a little excitement in her life"

For the next hour, we sat and talked about everything. It was so easy to talk to him and we had a lot in common. We both have a love for books and we are home bodies. Alex was telling me about all the places he has seen and the things he has done. For someone so young he's been to many exotic places. I was just about to ask him what he did for a living when I was interrupted by the DJ. "Ya'll know who it is! Fella's go ahead and get that dance dog!" shouted the DJ as a slow Hip Hop beat began to play.

"Yoooo! This is "Go Time" by BH! This is my shit, come on let's dance" replied Alex as he took me by the hand.

"Oh no, I don't dance"

"Weren't you the one looking for some excitement?

He led me to the center of the dance floor, where we were surrounded by the crowd of party goers. My heart was racing like a little hummingbird. I was nervous and yet excited at the same time. Everyone was watching us. He pulled me close as he wrapped his arm around my waist. He looked into my eyes as he said in his calm, low baritone voice, "Don't be nervous, it's just me and you on the dance floor".

Now I knew we weren't the only ones on the dance floor but it suddenly felt like we were alone. It was like I was compelled to believe him and I did. I put my arms around his neck as we slow danced to the music. Our bodies bumped and grind against each other to the baseline of the beat. I let one hand travel from his neck down his arm, slowly running my hand across his large bicep to his forearm. For the first time, I was lost in the moment, not worrying about what others might think, I just enjoyed the moment. The smell of his cologne, the heat from his body, his strong yet gentle touch, everything was intoxicating and I wanted more. He looked into my eyes as our bodies were intertwined, I felt he wanted to kiss me, hell I wanted him to kiss me. His lips looked so soft. He started to lean into me as I braced myself and closed my eyes. His face was so close to mine I could feel him breathing on me. Goosebumps ran down my spine as I anticipated his kiss. His lips were inches away from mine then he whispers in my ear, "Your friend has been gone for a while?"

When I opened my eyes, the crowd had made a circle around us. They had been watching us dance. I would have been embarrassed if it wasn't for the fact that Eve had been gone for a long time.

"I'm sorry it's getting late, and as you stated, my friend hasn't come back yet."

"I totally understand, you should check on her."

"Well it was nice meeting you, and thanks for the dance."

"The pleasure was all mine; maybe I'll see you around sometime."

"I would like that" I said as I unconsciously twirl my ponytail with my index finger. He took my hand and kissed it. I don't know what time period he thinks this is but I love it! I've only read about guys doing things like that. It's like he stepped right out the pages of one of my favorite romance novels. I was blushing, smiling from ear to ear. He let my hand go as he replied, "Shouldn't you be looking for your friend?"

"Oh yeah" I stuttered, still in a daze. I turned to start walking away as I thought to myself, "Maybe I should give him my number?" I turned back around to do just that but he was gone. Just like before, he disappointed, leaving me alone, wondering who he really was. Crestfallen, I set off in search of Eve. I headed towards the house in the direction Jag took her.

When I entered the home, it was eerily silent. As I stood in the large vaulted foyer, I could faintly hear the sound of a woman moaning followed by a slight giggle.

That had to be Eve and Jag. I slowly marched towards the sounds of their voices that echoed through the cavernous home. Their voices led me up a flight of spiral stairs. Before I made my way up the steps, Eve and Jag emerged from one of the rooms. I stopped, hiding behind the wall. Eve was leading Jag by the hand when he reversed their positions, pushing her up against the wall. He started kissing and caressing her. I couldn't help but think to myself, "Nigga didn't y'all just leave the room?" Then I started imagining that was Alex and I. Wait what was I thinking, I just met him, but that didn't stop my mind from drifting off.

My fantasizing was interrupted by the sound of Jags voice. He asked Eve if she loved him and if she wanted to be with him forever as she replied yes. He kissed her passionately, placing his hands gently on her face and with a quick flick of the wrist he snapped her neck. It took me a moment to realize what had happened as he held Eve's lifeless body in his arms. When I finally put two and two together I let out scream that rivaled that of a screeching banshee. Jag looked up at me with wide eyes; he didn't come after me cause his hands were occupied holding the corpse of my best friend. Without hesitation, I bolted down the spiral steps fearing for my life. I needed to find help and the first person that came to mind was the too tight t-shirt doorman. So, I sprinted for the entrance where I last saw him.

I found him outside on his phone. I frantically told him what I saw and I needed his help. He told whoever he was talking to that he would take care of it then hung up. "Okay calm down and show me…." Before he could say another word, I grabbed him by the arm and yanked his massive body behind me. We rushed back to where Jag had killed my best friend. When we made it back up the steps Jag and Eve were gone.

"They were right here" I said in a panic. I pushed open the door to the room Jag and Eve emerged from before he killed her. I tore that room apart looking for them. Mr. too tight t-shirt just stood in the doorway watching me like I was crazy. "Doesn't seem like anyone is here" he said in a condescending tone. I went to the next room to continue my search knowing they were gone. I must have been so focused on what happened to Eve I didn't notice too tight t-shirt man was standing behind me.

Before I could turn around, he wrapped a wire around my neck. Using the garrote, he lifted me off the ground as the wire dug deep into the flesh of my neck. I tried to grab hold of the wire but I couldn't get my fingers between the wire and my flesh. My feet were dangling in the air as I struggled to get free. I was desperate and running out of time. My lungs were screaming for a taste of oxygen. Darkness was creeping around the edges of my consciousness, panicking, I swung my legs in a backwards kicking motion. I made contact with his private area. He let out a scream of agony as his grip loosened, letting my body fall crashing to the floor.

I began coughing as my lungs tried to consume large quantities of oxygen. I got back on my feet while too tight t-shirt man was on his knees holding himself. My first instinct was to run. But I was so furious I ran up to him grabbed him by his ears and kneed him square in the face. The sound of his nose breaking and his screams echoed through the room as I tried to drive my knee through his face. He grabbed his nose trying to stop the bleeding. Before I made a mad dash for the door I punched him in the face and kicked him again in the nuts for good measure.

I ran for the door, sprinting down the hallway. I made my way down the stairs as quickly as I could. I was several feet away from the exit when I heard three thunderous booms followed by heat and excruciating pain as my body was spun around as I collapsed to the ground. I had been shot. I've read about it but to feel it was a different story. With every heartbeat, I could feel the warmth of my blood spread beneath me. The bullets went straight through my back and out my chest and stomach. One of the bullets must have hit my lungs because I was struggling to breathe as I coughed up blood. Too tight t-shirt man was walking towards me holding a massive hand cannon. As he stood above me, yelling, calling me a stupid bitch, as blood and spit flew from his mouth.

I couldn't believe this was how I was going to die. Tears fell from my eyes as I realized I would die alone. I closed my eyes as i began to pray that the lord would save me, but I knew that wasn't how prayers worked. I shouldn't pray only when I needed him but all the time so why would he answer my prayers now. So, I just prayed, thanking him for all the things he had done for me. Afterwards I was at peace as I looked up at too tight t-shirt man pointing his gun at my head. As I awaited the inevitable, a shadowy figure flew over me, snatching too tight t-shirt man away like he was a rag doll. I couldn't see anything all I could hear was screaming and gunshots followed by complete silence.

I was losing a lot of blood and could feel myself slipping into the darkness. From the floor, I could feel the vibration of someone walking in my direction. They stood over me but I couldn't make out who it was. I knew it wasn't too tight t-shirt man because this person wasn't that tall or wide. With the little strength I had left, I reached out with my hand as I tried to speak but no words came out. as I started losing consciousness; a hand reached out grabbing my mine. It was a strong hand with a gentle touch. It felt fa…mil...iar..…

EPISODE 2

"WHEN REALITY STRIKES"

I jumped up gasping for air clutching my chest. My heart was racing and I was breathing heavily. I calmed down as I noticed I was back at home lying on my couch. "What the hell is going on," I thought to myself. I had on my lounging clothes and was covered by a throw. Grabbing my glasses off the coffee table, I looked around the room to see if anyone was here but I was alone. I jumped off the couch running to the bathroom to look in the mirror. Everything was blurry so I reached up to make sure I had indeed put on my glasses. I lifted up my glasses from my nose; everything was clear, crystal clear. Sliding my glasses back on and everything was blurry again. "Something weird is going on" I thought. I took off the glasses to examined myself. There were no signs of being strangled. I snatched up my shirt to find there were no signs of bullet wounds. Now that I thought about it, I felt amazing. Then I thought of Eve, so I ran back to the couch, leaped over it landing on my feet. I grabbed my phone off the coffee table and called Eve. I was anxiously waiting as the phone rang hoping that she answered, but the voicemail picked up, so I left a message on her voicemail saying," Girl I just had the craziest dream, call me when you get this."

I hung up the phone and plopped down on the couch. "That dream felt so real…" I contemplated before another realization hit me, "wait, did I just jump over the couch?" Anyway, I was certain that I was dying last night. The memories of that moment were too fresh to be just a dream. On the other hand, meeting an attractive man with similar interest as me at some random party could have only been a dream. I drifted back into my memories of that dream and I could still feel his touch, hear his voice I can even smell his cologne….

I know I wasn't going crazy. I inhaled deeply, it was faint but I could smell his cologne on me. What the hell is going on here? Did that really happen or am I still dreaming? I was confused; my mind unable to tell what was real or not.

With a hundred and one things running through my mind, my train of thought was interrupted by the sound of two male voices. I looked around the house but it wasn't coming from inside my apartment. Now that the two voices had my attention I started to pick up their scent. I could smell alcohol on one of them like he mixed whiskey in his morning coffee and he wore the cheapest cologne that made my nose tingle. I could hear their footsteps getting louder and louder as they approached my door. I walked over to the door and stood in front of it. Once they reached my door I could hear their heartbeat, both steady and strong. Before they could knock I opened the door.

"Can I help you?" I asked curiously. The detectives looked at each other with a surprised expression. One of the detectives was dressed in regular street clothes, brown skin, with a mustache straight from the 70's, and a body like the penguin from The Batman comics. His partner was the total opposite. He was slim with a runner's build, dressed in a brown suit jacket, white button up shirt, blue jeans and brown boots. He had no facial hair on his long face.

The slim built detective said, "Yes ma'am. I'm detective Brian Johnson and this is my partner detective

Michael Brown. Are you Raven McCloud?" "That's me," I replied still not sure what was going on.

"Ms. McCloud, we have a few questions in regards to a party you attended last night. Could you come with us Downtown, please?"

"So, I did go to the party last night? Is Eve really dead and why and am I not dead or show any signs of injury," I thought to myself. Realizing I haven't responded to the detective's questions I asked, "Am I under arrest?"

"No ma'am, but we have a few questions, if you could just please come with me" replied Detective Johnson.

I thought about it for a moment. "Ok let me grab my things" I told the detectives as I grabbed my jacket. I locked the door behind me, then followed the detectives to their car. As I was getting in the back of the squad car, I couldn't help but feel like someone was watching me. I looked around but didn't see anyone so I got in the car, then we proceeded towards downtown.

They had me sitting a small room with no windows. The walls were painted an ugly institution green. The table that I sat at was made of some cheap metal and so was the chair I sat in. Sitting across from me was Detective Johnson, while his chubby partner stood in the corner behind him trying to look intimidating. I still had no idea what I was being questioned about.

"Where were you last night around 1:25am Ms. McCloud", asked Detective Johnson. I thought about it for a second because I honestly thought I was at a party but woke up at home, so I replied with the only logical answer, "I was at home reading"

Detective Johnson looked back at his partner who was shaking his head as if he was disappointed with my answer. Detective Johnson looked back at me, "Are you sure?" Now I'm nervous. Did I go out last? But if I did why am I not dead? I started rubbing my forehead, "Yes I'm sure" I said still unsure.

Detective Johnson slid a folder across the table. "Last night there was a homicide at a private party up in the hills. Security cameras place you at the scene of the crime"

I opened the folder to find pictures of me at the party entering the house. My heart started pounding as I looked through the pictures and then that's when I saw it. The next pictures were of too tight t-shirt man. My hands started to tremble as tears formed in my eyes. "This can't be possible", I softly said to myself.

"The victim was found dead in the foyer with what appears to have been attack by some type of animal. Did you see anything? Based on the video you would be the last person seen in or out of the home."

"It wasn't a dream?"

"Is there something you want to tell us?"

"I was at the party. I was there with my friend. We were invited by her boyfriend. They went into the home while I was left outside at the party by myself. It was getting late and she didn't return so I went to go find her. I entered the house and found them in the upstairs hallway and that's...."

I suddenly became emotional because if last night really happened then that means Eve is dead. Tears started falling down my face.

With that revelation, the words spilled out of me. "He killed her! I ran for help. The security guard came with me so I could show him what I seen but he tried to kill me. He was strangling me but I broke free. I tried to run but before I could get away he shot me. I thought I was going to die. Then I woke up at home this morning on my couch."

The two detectives stared at me as if my story was hard to believe. Chubby Detective Brown made his way to where detective Johnson and I were sitting and slammed his hands on the table as he shouted, "Lady that's some bullshit and you know it! You killed that guy!"

"Calm down Mike!" yelled Detective Johnson.

"Come on man, she wants us to believe that bullshit story? Man, fuck that she did it!"

Trying to fight back more tears I yelled, "It's true." The tears just continued to fall down my face. Detective Johnson reached in his jacket pocket pulling out some tissue. He handed them to me so I could dry my eyes.

"Now Ms. McCloud, as you can imagine, this is very hard to believe. Your story does explain the blood we found at the scene which didn't belong to the victim. If it is your blood then, why aren't you showing any signs of injury? You're completely unharmed."

I sat there in silence for a moment trying to understand the events from last night. I just couldn't understand why I wasn't dead or why I didn't have any wounds. Just as I thought I was about to make sense of this whole thing the door to the interrogation room opened. We all looked towards the door as a tall, dark and handsome man entered the room. The detectives had no idea who he was but I definitely recognized him. It was him, the guy from the party last night, Alex. "What the hell is going on?" is all I kept thinking to myself.

He wasn't dressed anything like he was yesterday. He had on a black leather jacket, a grey hoodie underneath it, blue jeans and some all black sneakers. He looked at me and winked as he addressed the two detectives.

"Alright that's enough questions for my client. She has had a difficult night and doesn't need to be harassed by the likes of you two." Detective Brown walks up on Alex who is a couple inches taller than him, "Who the hell do you think you are?" shouted Detective Brown.

Alex grabbed him by his collar with one hand and lifted his chubby body off his feet. He looked Detective Brown in his eyes then said, "Take your fat ass over there in that corner and don't say another word!" Alex put him back on his feet and like a mindless puppet Detective Brown walked towards the corner and didn't say a word. Detective Johnson sprang up from the table to confront Alex.

"What the hell did you do to my partner," replied Detective Johnson concerned for his partner. Before Detective Johnson could say another word, Alex placed his hand on the detective's shoulder looking him in the eyes. With a calm and ominous tone Alex spoke.

"You are to release Raven to me with all evidence associated with this case and with her." Detective Johnson started repeating Alex's exact words. His voice was similar to someone who was in a trance. Detective Johnson exited the room leaving Alex, me and Detective Brown in the interrogation room. I still have no idea what the hell was going on. Alex walked over to me and kneeled down in front of me. Holding my hands in his, "I know you have a lot of questions, I promise to explain once we get out of here"

I was speechless. I was happy to see him but if he was real then that means….

Before I could finish the thought, Detective Johnson returned holding a box labeled "Case number 58651-Evidence." Alex stood up and took the box from Detective Johnson. "Thank you", Alex said with a smile. He told me to stand at the door then he sat Detective Johnson and Detective Brown down at the dented metal table in the center of the room. In that same calm and low tone Alex spoke.

"Once we leave this room you will forget everything that has happened in the last 24hrs that involves Raven and myself. You will go back to doing your normal cop routine" The two detectives nodded their heads in acknowledgment. I don't know how he was doing it but it was amazing and a little creepy. Alex finally turned towards me and with a smile and said, "Let me get that door for you." He opened the door and gestured for me to exit. Before he left the room, he turned back to address the detectives one last time.

"Oh, and one more thing fat boy, get on a diet and cut that damn mustache off your face. You're a cop not a damn 70's porn star." I couldn't help but smile. It was funny and true; Detective Brown did have an ugly mustache.

Alex was the first out of the precinct with me following not too far behind. Now that I was out of that building and no longer worried about going to jail, reality sank in. Last night really happened. Alex was heading towards an old school muscle car. I couldn't tell you what it was all I know is it was all black and it looked vicious. He looked back at me as I was still standing on the steps of the precinct.

"Who are you?'

"Let me give you a ride and I'll try to explain.'

"How did you find me?"

"Just get in the car, Raven."

I stood there for a moment weighing my options, like I really had any. I walked to the car; as he came to the passenger side and opened the door for me. Alex closed my door then he got in the car and then we drove off. For the first couple minutes we rode in silence, only the rumbling of the engine could be heard. We came to a light and stopped. Alex turned to me and said, "I know you have a million questions, I promise I'll explain everything, but right now, I just need you to trust me. It's not safe for you to be by yourself right now."

Staring at him I said, "You're the guy from last night. How did you find me and what the hell do you do back there?"

"Yes, it's me, aaaaaaaand it's kind of hard to explain the rest. You wouldn't believe me anyway."

"Try me. After the night I've had and what I just saw, it can't get any more unbelievable than that. At this point I'm pretty open-minded.

Alex looked at me then took a deep breath. "Ok, don't say I didn't warn you. Last night I was tracking down a vampire. I was on his trail until I saw you were in trouble. I also took care of the man who shot you, then I saved you and that was that."

"Wait! You're telling me I really was dying last night!? Then why am I not dead?"

"I told you, I saved you."

"How?!"

Alex didn't respond he didn't even look at me he just kept driving. I started to get angry. I've never felt this type of rage. Before I knew it, I yelled out, "HOW!"

Alex slammed on the brakes bringing the car to a screeching halt.

"I BIT YOU OK! You were lying in a puddle of your own blood dying, begging for your life so I bit you. I'm surprised the bite didn't kill you.

"You bit me?" I thought to myself. "What do you mean you bit me", I said curiously.

"So, you want me to believe that vampires exist and you're one of them?" Alex started driving again. "I never said I was a vampire, but yes, they do exist and that's why you are in danger" said Alex returning to a calmer tone. I still was having a hard time believing him but how else am I to explain last night's events.

"So, that's the story you want me to believe? I knew you were too good to be true. The attractive ones are always the crazy ones."

"Let me ask you something Raven. Have you noticed anything different about yourself lately? Like improved hearing and sight? "How is your sense of smell?"

I thought about what he asked. I mean I no longer need my glasses and I can see much better without them. I remembered hearing and smelling the detective before they ever reached my front door. I all around felt different, in a good way. But I wasn't ready to accept the existence of vampires that's just crazy talk.

"Alright, I've had enough crazy talk for one day. You can just let me out...."

"I told you, you wouldn't believe me"

"Vampires, really?"

"Would you prefer that I told you this is all a dream, because I assure you what happened last night, was real. Hell, me being here now should be proof enough.

I wasn't ready to accept what happened last night was real. Because if I did then that means Eve was really...

"Ok I've heard enough stop the car."

"No can do little lady, you are my responsibility and I say you're safer with me"

I don't know what happened next but something inside me snapped. I could feel myself getting angry. It wasn't that he wouldn't let me out the car. It was everything that just happened. Realizing that last night wasn't a dream, not being able to help my friend and feeling powerless, the memories of the pain I felt as I laid there dying. The fact that Eve is really…. Before I could finish the thought, I could feel a heat deep in my stomach and it was rising up through my body. I was trying to contain my anger but I could feel it creeping out of me like steam from tea pot. I don't know if it was my imagination or not but I could hear the sound of an animal growling in my head. Alex must have heard it too because he looked over at me with wide eyes.

"I said LET ME OUT NOW!"

Alex pulled over and parked the car. I was breathing heavily as I forced the car door open and exited the vehicle.

"Hey, before you go take this" Alex hands me a matte black business card with Japanese characters on it in a high gloss black finish. "Just in case you get in trouble I'll be able to find you."

I took the card and started to walk away. I could feel him watching me but I didn't want to look back because if I did I would have gotten back into the car. After a moment, he finally drove off. Ugh what's happening to me! I just pushed away the only guy interested in my well-being. I can't believe

I walked away from his cute self. After my anger finally settled down I realized it was already getting dark and I was just a few blocks from Eve's apartment. If I didn't die last night maybe she is still alive too. I have to believe she is alright for my sake. With new found hope, I headed to Eve's hoping to find her lying in her bed. So, I started running. I started out in a light jog, but I felt I could go faster so I picked up the pace. The evening air felt amazing on my face as I ran. I still felt like I could go faster so I decided to go full sprint. I inhaled deep filling my lungs with oxygen and with one forceful push I was gone. I could hear my ponytail cutting through the evening air as I moved effortlessly down the block. It took me only minutes to clear the several blocks it took to get to Eve's house. When I reached her complex, I wasn't winded at all. I felt great.

    I don't know what happened to me but I could get use to this. I reached into my pocket for my keys. Yes, I have a key to her house; we wouldn't be best friends if I didn't. I unlocked the main door and took the elevator to the third floor. Eve stayed in apartment 3c. I exited the elevator making my way to her door. I had been to Eve's place hundreds of times. Yet, this time was completely different. In the hallway, I was overwhelmed by all the different smells. It smelled like everyone was cooking at the same time then tried to mask the scent with some cheap air freshener. I rushed into Eve's apartment slamming the door behind me. Eve's apartment was completed dark but I was still able to see in the darkness. I found a lamp and flipped the switch on. The apartment looked like your typical female's home; a bunch of cute and fuzzy things everywhere decorated in bright colors with dozens of extra pillows on the couch, chairs and floor, while the walls had cute portraits of us from throughout the years. As I walked through the home I realized she wasn't here. I checked the bedroom and it was a mess as usual but no Eve.

    Disappointed that she wasn't here like I hoped, I walked to the kitchen to get something to eat. I don't know if it was the full-on sprint I just did but I was starving. I opened the fridge and she didn't really have anything to eat. The only thing I found was a leftover steak from some fancy restaurant she went to. I took the leftovers and popped them in the microwave for a couple minutes. Once it was finished cooking I took it, grabbed a bottle of water and made my way to the couch. I took a bite from the steak which was medium rare and delicious. As I continued eating I couldn't help but hope that Eve was ok, she had to be ok.

EPISODE 3

"A WHOLE NEW WOLRD"

Jag sat in a wing-backed chair at the foot of a king size sleigh bed. He had been watching his beloved lay in the bed for the past twenty-four hours. Normally when he turned someone it never took this long and that had him worried. Did he give her his blood before snapping her delicate neck? The suspense of waiting was getting to him. He hopped up from his chair and started pacing back and forth in his master bed room. He placed his hands on his freshly shaven bald head as he thought the worst. Just as he was about to lose hope, his beloved finally awoke. She jumped up from the bed gasping for air like someone had been holding her underwater.

She looked around the room and was unfamiliar with her surroundings. All she knew was that she was in someone's bedroom. Then she saw her boyfriend standing next to the doorway. He made his way to the bed as he sat next to her. She could see the relief on his face as if he has been worrying all night.

"How do you feel my darling" he said as he caressed her leg. Eve started rubbing her neck. It felt kind of stiff as if she slept wrong.

"I feel fine, what happened last night?"

"Tell me what you remember."

"Uum I remember going to the party with Raven. I remember you and me going somewhere to be alone. You told me you loved me and wanted us to be together forever. I told you I felt the same way, then we kissed and… You muthafucka!"

"Baby calm down let me explain……"

Eve became furious at the realization that her loving boyfriend tried to kill her. Filled with rage Eve slapped Jag in the face sending him hurling across the room, slamming into the wall then crashing to the floor with a thunderous thud. She stared, stunned. She was in shock and confused. Eve looked down at her neatly manicured hands, "What did you do to me" she yelled. Jag was getting to his feet as he started to softly laugh, "I made it so we can be together forever."

"Nigga what do you mean you made it so we can be together forever?"

"I gave you the gift of eternal life, and at this very moment you are going through the transition phase"

Eve started to get angrier as she moved towards Jag, "Fool if you don't start making sense I swear to god!" Jag feared she would hit him again and didn't want to cause her any harm so he blurted out in a nervous tone, "I'm a vampire and I made you just like me." Eve frowned up her face. She couldn't believe the bullshit her boyfriend was trying to sale her. "Nigga is you high?"

He closed his eyes and took a deep breath. Eve was still looking at him with confusion. However, when he opened his eyes they shimmered, an emerald green color. He gave Eve a smile that revealed his fangs. "You believe me now?" He could see her face go from confused to complete terror. She snatched her hands from his and in a blink of an eye she went from standing in front of him to the opposite corner of the room.

"Oh, shit you really are a vampire!" In her moment of terror, Eve didn't realize how fast she had moved clear across the room. She tried to leave the room but every time she tried, Jag would appear in front of her, blocking her exit.

"Eve just calm down and let me help you" Jag grabbed her and pulled her close to him. She tried to break free from his hold but was unable to. She kept screaming for him to let her go. He placed her head on his chest. "Just take deep breaths, relax and focus on the sound of my heartbeat." Eve continued to struggle to break free but the sound of Jags heartbeat gradually started to catch her attention. The more she focused on the gentle beat of his heart the calmer she became until she was completely calm. They stood in the middle of the master bedroom holding each other.

"Do you feel better now?" asked Jag. Eve nodded her head yes. "Now I'm going to let you go, only if you promise not to attack me or try to run off?" Eve replied by nodding her head yes. Jag let her go and she went to sit down on at the foot of the bed. Jag followed and sat beside her.

"I thought vampires had to bite you to turn you?" said Eve still trying to understand what was happening to her.

"There are a lot of myths and folklore in regards to vampires. Being bit by a vampire to be turned is a total myth.

To be turned you must drink the blood of a vampire and die with their blood in your system. It was designed this way so that turning someone into a vampire was by selection not by a bite. If that was the case, there would be way more vampires in the world."

"But I don't remember drinking your blood."

Jag starts to look guilty. "I may have slipped my blood in your drink last night."

"You slipped me a vampire date rape drug?" Eve pushed Jag away from her.

"Ok, I know I should've asked, but if I told you I was a vampire would you have believed me? Besides you said you wanted us to be together forever so I thought you'd be cool with it."

Eve thought about it, and she agreed she would never believe no crazy mess about him being a vampire. "Well when someone says they want to be with you forever it usually means marriage not turning someone into a vampire. So, now what?"

"Now you must complete the transition phase."

"Ok and how do I do that?"

"You must drink the blood of a human."

Eve is disgusted by the notion of drinking blood, "Drink blood? Ugh, what if I don't?"

"Then you will die."

Eve sits there for a moment contemplating her next move. She knows it's a no brainer but the thought of drinking blood just seems so gross to her.

"Well a bitch like me ain't ready to die yet. So, give me some blood so I can get this over with" said Eve filling Jags heart with joy. He grabbed Eve by the hand, escorting her downstairs to the kitchen. In the center of the kitchen was an island. He pulled out a stool for her to have a seat. The kitchen was very modern and clean. It looked like this was the first time the kitchen had ever been used. Jag opened the refrigerator and grabbed a wine bottle. He then went to the cabinet to grab two wine glasses then made his way to the island where Eve was patiently waiting. He sat a glass in front of her. Jag took the bottle and popped the cork. The scent of blood emanated from the bottle as Eve began to salivate.

"Is that what I think it is?" asked Eve as she watched, now anxious for a taste. Jag smiled as he pours her a glass of blood filling her cup only half way.

"Yes, this is human blood".

"I was expecting to drink it out of one of those blood donor bags, but this is fancier."

"Normally you would but this is a special occasion for my special lady", Jag poured himself a glass and sat the bottle on the island countertop. As Jag poured his glass of blood Eve was staring at her glass as if lost in a trance. She almost felt as if the blood was calling to her like a whisper. Jag raised his glass," Let's make a toast, to love and eternal life."

Eve raised her glass, tapping her glass against Jags glass. Jag proceeded to drink his glass of blood. Eve looked at her glass still hesitant to drink. She started to hear the whispers again. It was too faint to tell what it was actually saying; all she knew was that it was enticing her to drink. She finally gave into the whispers. She gently placed the glass on her lips, pouring the blood slowly into her mouth. The blood danced on her taste buds. She had never tasted anything like it. No longer afraid, she drank the rest of the blood vigorously.

Leaning her head back making sure she got every drop of blood in the glass. As the last drop of blood touched her soft lips, Eve fell into a trance, lost in ecstasy. She closed her eyes as she ran her hands through her hair and caressed her face. A drop of blood was trickling down the side of her mouth. She took her thumb and wiped the blood from her face. She licked the blood from her thumb revealing her brand-new fangs.

Jag was watching the entire time slightly aroused. When Eve opened her eyes, they were a luminesce emerald green. "That was amazing", she replied in a seductive voice.

"Well if you liked that, then wait until you taste it straight from the vein"

"Oh, really? Let's go!!"

"Slow down little lady, one step at a time. First you need to learn a few things. Don't want you to turn into some blood lusting monster."

"Ok. Well, teach me"

Jag grabbed Eve's glass to pour her another glass of blood then poured himself one. "Well, let's start with the basics. Vampires need to feed on humans to survive. As long as you feed and stay out of the gaze of the sun, you will live forever. Since I'm on the topic of what can kill you, a wooden stake to the heart will kill you too, oh and a bite from a werewolf will kill you. Now that's the worst way to go."

"Wait, you telling me werewolves exist too...."

"Yes and witches there is an entire community of supernatural beings."

"Uuum…ok. Let's just stick with vampires for now. Were you born a vampire?" asked Eve curiously as she sipped her wine glass of blood.

"No, I was turned into a vampire back in 1845. Along with having super strength and speed, you have the ability to compel humans to do your bidding…."

"Oh, you have to teach me how to compel, I'm sure that's going to come in handy."

"I'll teach you that and much more…."

"Did you say 1845?? That makes you over 150 years old! Damn you're old!"

Jag gives Eve a faint laugh, "In the Vampire Nation, 150yrs old is pretty young. The older the vampire the stronger that vampire is. Now the vampire who turned my brothers and me is one of the oldest vampires, Lord Solomon. He was born a vampire, pureblood, a blue blood..."

"Wait you have brothers? Where are all these vampires hiding?

"Yes, I have brothers. We weren't born brothers. Lord Solomon turned us all and adopted us as his own sons, and we vampires have been living in the Vampire District peacefully among humans. Lord Solomon created a place for vampires to live here in the city."

"Where is this Vampire District?"

"Where do you think we are now?"

"I'm in the District now?

"You know what, come on...

"Where are we going?"

Jag grabs his car keys and then takes Eve by the hand. "Instead of trying to explain it to you, it's just better if you see for yourself." He escorts her to the garage and opens the door to his luxury coupe. Eve gets in and he closes the door. He gets in the car starts the engine. The rumble of his exotic coupe bounced off the walls of the garage with a thunderous sound. He backed out the garage and down the driveway slowly. When he finally hit the street, he put the car in drive and shot down the road like a rocket. The force made Eve's neck jerk slightly.

Eve looked out her window as Jag races through the neighborhood. Jag slowly approaches what appears to be a security gate. The security guard looks out the window of his tiny office. Jag gives him a slight head nod as he pulls out an id card and waves it up against a small black box. The box made an electronic beep then the large black scrolled wrought iron gate began to open. The hydraulics whispered as the gate slowly opened. Jag didn't wait for the gate to open completely. As soon as he had enough space to squeeze through the gate he slammed on the gas. The tires screamed as he burned rubber zooming off barely clearing the gate.

"What's with the gate?" said Eve as she clenched in her seat.

"That's where the upper-class vamps stay, the rest of the vampires live in regular neighborhoods just like humans."

They continued their tour through the Vampire district. The area looked like your normal everyday neighborhood.

They have convenient stores with guys hanging on the corner and everything, the only thing different was it was all vampires.

"So, everybody here is a vampire? But there are so many!"

"This is just the tip of the iceberg; The Vampire nation is vast"

"So, what happens during the day? Does everyone stay in the house?"

"Oh no, Lord Solomon had a group of witches cast a spell that protects us from the sun. It's basically a giant dome of eternal night. It also keeps unwanted guest from entering the District. So, if you aren't invited then you will not be able to enter."

Jag starts to slow down. He parked the car at the end of a long and abandoned road. He exits the car as Eve follows after him.

"This is the edge of the barrier." replied Jag.

They walked towards the end of the barrier. As they came closer, Eve could see something in front of her starting to wave and ripple like a body of water. The closer she got the more she could see the transparent barrier. She extended her hand to touch the barrier as her hand went right through it. The barrier rippled outwards from where her hand made contact. The waves expanding outward like a pebble being dropped into a pound. Eve looked back at Jag; he nodded at her, letting her know everything was ok. She turned back around to continue walking through the barrier. When she got past the barrier, she found herself in an abandoned construction site. Excited, she turned back to look at Jag but couldn't see him because he was hidden behind the barrier. All she could see was the rest of the abandoned construction site.

Moments later Jag emerged from the barrier. "This is how we keep humans from stumbling into the District"

"This is amazing! Do the other supernatural live in hiding like this?"

"No, werewolves and witches live among the humans. They don't feed on humans like we do. To keep us from being hunted by hunters the District was created. Werewolves have their packs, witches have their covens and we have the Vampire Nation"

"Oh ok", said Eve.

"I know it's a lot to take in. Let's go back to the house so you can get some rest."

"I'm fine. I just realized I left Raven alone at the party. I know she's probably worried sick."

Jag looked shocked when he heard Ravens name because he knew something Eve did not. He had sent someone to take care of Raven...permanently. "Oh, baby, don't worry about that. I had one of my guys take care of her. She's fine", said Jag with a nervous chuckle.

"Well, can I use your phone to call her to let her know I'm alright?"

Before Jag could come up with another lie his cell phone rang. "Hold that thought baby", he replied feeling relieved he was saved by the bell. When he answered the phone, the man on the other line was very upset and angry. The man proceeded to tell Jag that one of their men was found dead last night at the house party, and he appeared to have been attacked by a werewolf. Jag replied, "How did a werewolf get past security?"

The man continued to tell Jag that the girl the guard was supposed to "take care of" was also missing. Engrossed in the conversation, Jag is startled when Eve interrupts.

"If I can't call her, can we at least go to my house so I can grab some things?"

Jag takes his ear away from the phone and covers it with his hand, "I'm sorry baby something just came up, that needs my immediate attention. What I'll do is have one of my guy's grab some things for you"

"Uh, I don't want any random man in my house"

"I understand baby, but it ain't safe for you to be out there right now. You know what...I'll stop by there myself, ok?"

"Ok, since I don't really have a choice."

Jag and Eve start walking back through the barrier towards the car. As they rode back to Jags house Eve couldn't help but wonder if her best friend was ok.

"I can't believe he has us running errands for his girl", said one of Jag's henchmen as he sat in the passenger seat of an all-black SUV parked outside of an apartment complex. "I mean look at this fucking list? Who this bitch thinks she is? The Princess of Zumunda or something?"

"Watch ya mouth! That's the bosses lady you talking about!" said the driver aggressively. "Let's just get her shit so we can go."

"Man fuck all this! Let's just find us a few humans to feed on, better yet let's go down to Dorian's!"

"I'm not trying to have them guild hunters after me and especially not that scary ass Phantom Hunter for killing a human, and you know good damn well only vampire high society knows where Dorian's is"

The two men exited the vehicle, making their way into the apartment. They walked down the hallway towards the elevator, looking left and right, checking their surroundings to ensure no one was watching. One of them pressed the up button, calling the elevator to creep down from the third floor. The elevator reached the first floor, chiming before the doors opened. The two men entered the elevator, pressing the button for the third floor. The two henchmen rode the elevator quietly contemplating their next moves. The elevator bell dinged as the doors opened. The two men exited the elevator, heading towards apartment 3c.

"Ugh! I'm tired of running these dumb ass errands. Don't you ever want to do something exciting with these vampire powers besides being errand boys?" The driver looked at his friend shaking his head, "No, I don't mind it at all, we have an eternity. So, watch what you ask for, you just might get it. You see what happened to old boy at the party last night. He was killed."

"Yeah, I heard it was a werewolf. If that was me I would have whooped that wolf's ass!" said the driver's friend as he opened the door to apartment 3C. As they walked into the apartment they were surprised to find a young woman sitting on the couch eating a steak. She was a light skinned female with raven black hair pulled into a ponytail. She turned towards the door hoping to see her best friend but was disappointed to find it wasn't her.

The driver's friend recognized her from the party last night and shouted to his friend, "Oh shit! It's the bitch from last night!"

"Who…" said the driver in a confused tone.

"The bitch! The bitch from last night!!!"

Raven recognized them from last night as well and she became furious instantly. The driver's friend charged towards Raven as his eyes changed from dark brown to a glimmering emerald green as his fangs extended. The driver tried to stop his friend from attacking the young lady but he was snatched from the apartment doorway into the hallway. The driver couldn't move. He was being pinned up against the wall by a man using only one hand. The driver struggled to break free from this mysterious man who had him pressed against the wall. Even with his superior vampire strength he was helpless. This wasn't some ordinary man.

"Who the fuck is you!" yelled the driver as he continued to struggle to break free from the man's grasp.

"Oh, we can't have you joining the fun now can we!" said Alex, as he looked the man in his eye to compel him.

Inside the apartment Raven was furious, her rage was consuming her. Her breathing was heavy as her eyes changed from brown to a luminous yellow. Her manicured nails were now razor sharp claws and her pearly white teeth resembled that of an animal as her canine fangs extended. The driver's friend lunged at Raven. She caught him in mid-air then tossing him across the room, crashing into the wall then slamming onto the floor. Raven leapt over to the vampire who lay sprawled on the floor. She snatched him up by his collar and flung him towards the couch like he was a rag doll. The man hit the floor, sliding into the couch. He struggled to get back on his feet; before he could, Raven was all on him. She grabbed him by the neck lifting him in the air with one hand.

Holding him in the air by his neck, she asked, "Where is Eve?"

"Fuck you bitch" the vampire replied, he was barely able to speak as Raven squeezed the airways in his throat shut. She let out a low growl and with her free hand; she extended her claws preparing to rip out the vampire's heart. Just as she was about to thrust her clawed hand through the vampire's chest, someone grabbed her by the wrist. She turned her head quickly to find Alex holding her. Consumed by her rage she didn't even recognize him.

She threw the vampire she was holding to the ground unconscious, pointing her attention to Alex.

"Raven, that's enough" said Alex calmly but she just looked at him then roared. She tried to claw Alex's' face but he just dodged her attacks effortlessly.

"Raven snap out of it!"

Raven didn't respond, she continued her assault clawing at Alex as he avoided her every attempt.

"Alright, I didn't want to have to do this but you leave me with no choice. Here is your first lesson" said Alex to a rage consumed, savage Raven. Alex prepared himself for Ravens next attack. She lunged at him with claws extended. Alex side stepped letting Ravens momentum send her flying past him as she slammed into the wall. She looked back at Alex as she became more enraged, roaring with fury. This gave Alex enough distance between them to do what he needed.

"So, you want to roar? Let me show you what a real roar sounds like" he replied as Raven charged him. He didn't budge; he just closed his eyes, taking a deep breath. When he opened his eyes, they burned a bright ruby red. Once his lungs was filled with enough oxygen, he opened his mouth unleashing a roar that snatched Raven right out of her berserk mode, stopping her dead in her tracks as she covered her ears. The sound of his roar echoed not only in the building but throughout the city. It was heard so clear that it caught the attention of two werewolf hunters, one male and the other female, miles away sitting outside on their car talking and enjoying dinner. When they heard his roar, their eyes turned a luminous yellow as they looked in the direction the call was coming from. They looked at each other, and then immediately hopped in their car speeding off in the direction of the thunderous animal call.

Raven was standing in the center of Eve's apartment covering her ears with her eyes closed. When she opened them, they were no longer glowing yellow. She had completely returned to their normal form. Still dazed and confused, she looked around the apartment unable to remember what had happened or who destroyed her best friend's home.

"What the hell happened? Did I do this?" Raven gasped as Alex picked up the man she almost killed, putting him on the couch. Then Alex signaled the driver who was still standing at the door to come and have a seat as well. Raven recognized the two men from the party last night. She started to get angry again and Alex could sense it. He pointed at her and in a stern voice he said, "You, calm down!"

Raven noticed her anger and the feeling of her changing. She looked down at her hands as saw her claws retract as she calmed down, "What is happening to me?"

"We don't have much time. I'm pretty sure every super natural being in the area just heard my call. Someone is bound to be on their way to investigate"

"I'm really a werewolf?" exclaimed Raven still unable to comprehend what was happening to her.

"Yes and these two beauty queens are vampires. I'll explain later but first."

Alex kneels down on his knee to get eye level with the two vampires sitting on the couch; his eyes burned a bright ruby red, as Alex spoke in a calm low voice, "Where is her friend?"

"She is with Jag" replied the driver in a monotone voice.

"Is she alright?" shouted Raven.

"Answer her." barked Alex to the driver.

The driver nodded his head yes.

While Alex is getting information from the driver, the vampire Raven beat up is finally regaining consciousness.

"Ugh, Nigga what are you doing...."

Before he could finish his sentence, Alex reached over grabbing the vampire by the collar; turning to him the vampire looked into Alex's glowing red eyes, and in a calm yet forceful voice Alex barked, "Shut up!" The vampire fell silent. Alex returned his attention to the driver as Raven watched anxiously. She couldn't understand how Alex was controlling these vampires.

"Where are they now?"

"They are in the Vampire District" mumbled the Driver.

Alex was unpleased with the information he received. Suddenly he could hear the sound of a vehicle pulling up outside and the familiar scent of werewolves.

"We're out of time..." replied Alex.

With the two werewolves approaching, Alex had to move quickly. Looking them in their eyes and in a calm voice he spoke. "The two of you will forget ever seeing us once we leave."

Raven grabbed Alex by the shoulder, "What are you doing, they know where Eve is" she pleaded.

Alex stood up, grabbed Raven by the wrist, quickly pulling her towards the window. "No time, we're about to have visitors. We need to be gone before they get up here", replied Alex urgently.

Raven struggled to break free from Alex's grip. "I'm not leaving until they tell me where she is…."

Using one arm, Alex pulled Raven close to him so they were touching chest to chest. While Raven continued to pull and tug away from Alex, he could hear the elevator doors open. The sound of footsteps quickly approached the apartment. With no more time left to spare Alex placed two fingers on his forehead and in the blink of an eye they vanished.

Seconds later, a tall light skin female stepped into the apartment. With her gun drawn she approached the two vampires on the couch cautiously. Following behind her with his gun drawn as well was a male a little short than the female, a shade darker in complexion and with his hair in dreads. With her keen sense of smell she recognized the foul stench of vampire in the room. The two vampires finally started to come out of the hypnotic trance to find themselves looking down the barrel of a gun.

"Well look what we have here sis" said the male hunter as he held his gun pointed in the face of the driver.

"I hope you two have a pretty good explanation, because it's not looking good for you two" replied the female hunter.

The driver looked at his friend completely disgusted with their current situation, "You happy now?" he barked as his friend shook his head, lowering it in shame.

Alex and Raven appeared out of thin air landing in a large living room next to a huge open fireplace. The room had a very old Victorian décor. Alex finally released his grip on Raven as she pushed away from him. She was still furious with Alex.

"Let me go, I have to find Eve, LET ME GO!" shouted Raven as she examined the room with her eyes, realizing she was no longer in Eve's apartment. "Where are we? How did we get here?"

"Calm down Raven. Your friend is with vampires and that can only mean one of two things. Either she is on the menu or she has been turned. At this point, there is nothing you can do to help her, not until you can control yourself.

Alex's words caused Raven to become even angrier. She grabbed an antique looking vase off of the end table she was standing by and threw it into the fire place. "That's impossible! Eve would never do anything like that. Those monsters did this to her!"

"Look at yourself! You can't even control your anger. How are you going to help her and you can't even think straight to help yourself? Think about it! You said you saw her die. Then those two suck heads show up at her house telling you she is with their boss… a vampire."

Raven still didn't want to accept what Alex was telling her. "You can't keep me here!" She yelled as she sprinted out of the room, down a long hallway. Alex didn't give chase; he just let her run off. He looked into the fireplace where Raven threw the vase as he replied, "That was my vase"

When Raven reached the door, she snatched it open as she stepped outside. Shocked by her surroundings, she found herself standing on a path made of gravel that traveled down a massive yard. Green grass spread out before her as far as the eye could see. The cool tropical breeze brushed up against Ravens soft skin. She could smell the ocean in the air as she tried to make sense of what she was seeing. She knew good and well that she didn't live near an ocean. So, she started running down the gravel path. She reached the end of the trail only to find herself standing at the edge of a beach. She turned back towards the house to see the silhouette of a mansion against the evening sky. She grew even more frustrated, so she kept running. She ran the entire length of the estate until she finally realized that she was stranded on an island. Standing on an abandoned boat dock, Raven had tears of frustration forming in her eyes as she stared out into the endless expanse of ocean. A hand gently touched her on the shoulder. Raven turned around to find Alex standing there. She begins to cry even more.

Alex pulled Raven close, resting her head on his chest. "What am I supposed to do? I can't just sit around knowing my friend maybe in danger" she sobbed.

"Let me help you. I'll show you how to control your new powers and use them to get your friend back. Maybe even show you how to kill a few vampires along the way."

Raven nodded her head yes, never noticing the fact she was still in the arms of Alex. The sound of his beating heart mixed with the soothing sounds of the ocean calmed her, made her feel safe like everything would be alright.

"If it wasn't for the unfortunate chain of events, standing here in the arms of an attractive man looking out into the endless ocean on a deserted island would be so romantic" Raven thought to herself.

EPISODE 4

"GEORGIA 1845"

Deep in the woods of rural Georgia, a man draped in a black hooded cloak rides his ebony stallion slowly along the wooded trail. As they make their way through the endless mazes of trees, the sounds of men whooping and hollering fill the evening sky. The rider looked in the direction of the commotion to find the burning light of torches moving through the trees in the distance. Curious, the hooded man turns his steed towards the commotion, drawn to it like a moth to a flame.

When he caught up to them, he found five Caucasian males surrounding a shirtless African slave. The young black man looked no more than twenty-five years old. His body was covered with scars that were common signs of being beat with a whip. In his hand, he was gripping a large piece of wood.

The cloaked rider watched anxiously to see how things were going to unfold.

"We got you now boy" yelled one of the white men. "You don't sleep with your master's wife and think you live to tell about it. You a dead nigger now"

"I'm tired of running, if you going to kill me then get it over with. Just know I'm not going down without a fight" said the black man proudly as he held the large piece of wood like a bat ready to strike at any moment.

"Good, I like my nigger with a little fight in'em, makes this more fun" replied the white man.

The white men dropped their torches as they began to transform right in front of the young black man's eyes. The five white men started to grow claws and fangs as their eyes all started to glow a luminous yellow against the black evening sky. The young black man didn't know what was going on as these men turned into monsters before him. Watching from the shadows, the cloaked man knew what these men were. They were werewolves. The cloaked rider clutched his fist as he watched the inevitable happen.

The young black man was terrified but he made up his mind he would rather die fighting then live like a slave. The white men growled and howled at the young black man. One of the men, now turned beast lunged at the black man with claws extended. The black man swung his large piece of wood, smashing it on the side of the werewolf's face sending the beast crashing to the ground. He let out a loud dog yelp as his body hit the ground.

Enraged, the others attack the black man all at once. They slashed and clawed at the black man's legs, back and abdomen. The young man did all he could to protect himself but it was no use. He collapsed to the ground, blood oozing from his wounds. The five werewolves slowly circle his motionless body. The young man begins to move, slowly getting back on his feet using the piece of wood as a crutch to keep him upright.

"We got ourselves a tough nigger! Don't worry, I'll make your death quick boy" snarled one of the white man as blood dripped from his claws.

The black man could barely stand on his own feet, let alone fight off another attack from these beasts. The werewolf lets out a thunderous roar when suddenly he falls silent. The werewolf looks down at his chest to find a blade made of silver protruding from his chest. When he looked back, he found a man hidden under a black cloak holding the other end of the sword. The cloaked man lifted the werewolf off his feet. The werewolf coughs up blood as he is expanded in the air. The other wolfs look back to see a member of their pack being killed. The Cloaked man flung the werewolf to the side like he was nothing more than a rag doll.

The four remaining wolves howled for their fallen wolf. They turned their anger from the barely conscious black man who wasn't sure if what he was witnessing was real or his mind playing tricks on him due to the amount of blood loss. The Cloaked man walked in the center of the four wolves as they circled around him, his silver blade shimmered under the pale moonlight. Without warning the four werewolves attacked. The cloaked man dodged and maneuvered between the wolves' attacks at an uncanny speed as he chopped the werewolves down one by one until he was the only one standing.

The young man couldn't believe what he just seen. How did this man single handedly take down those monsters?

The cloaked man surrounded by his enemies' slaughtered bodies at his feet, bent down as he snatched the shirt off of one of the dead werewolves who had already returned to their human form. He used the cloth to wipe the blood off his silver blade. "Filthy mutts" he muttered to himself as he returned his shimmering silver blade back into its sheath.

The young man wanted to collapse, the pain from his wounds was starting to take their toll on him but he wasn't sure if he was still in danger or not. The cloaked man started to slowly make his way towards the young man. The young man couldn't see the cloaked man's face due to it being hidden under his hood. What he could see was a pair of glowing amber eyes looking at him. The young man tried the best he could to brace himself.

"No need to be afraid my child, I will cause you no harm" whispered the cloaked rider as he approach the young man. "What is your name my child"?

The young man was hesitant to speak then replied, "My name is Christian"

"Hmmm, I was watching you Christian. You showed no fear against these mutts. I could use a man of your character. Join me and I can give you great power"

"Power? What kind of power?" questions Christian curiously.

"The power so you don't have to run again, to be your own man"

Christian looked at what the cloaked man did to his attackers and wanted that power. He did not want to feel powerless again, he was tired of running, but with this mysterious man's help it could be possible.

"How can I join someone who hides himself?"

The cloaked rider titled his head as he looked at Christian. This man was barely holding on and yet he questioned him. The cloaked man knew he had chosen wisely. The cloaked rider nodded his head as he removed his hood. Christian couldn't believe his eyes. The cloaked man was like him, a black man. The cloaked man stood at six feet four inches tall. He had a bald head with smooth toasted cinnamon skin. He had no facial hair and his eyes shined the brightest of amber. "My name is Solomon White.

Christian never seen a black man with such power and he wanted it. Without hesitation Christian blurted out, "I'll join you" as he his legs finally gave out sending Christian collapsing to the ground. Solomon kneeled down to Christian as he tries to get back to his feet. Solomon rolled up his sleeve. Taking his long finger nail, he punctured the flesh of his wrist, causing his blue blood to run from his wound.

"Here, drink my child," demanded Solomon as he extended his arm to Christian.

Christian was hesitant, he never seen blue blood before, but he wanted his power. He took Solomon's wrist and drank deep. Christian could feel his wounds begin to heal as he regained his strength.

"What are you?" replied Christian, wiping the blue blood from his lips.

Solomon placed his hands gently on Christian's face, "I am a vampire and now you're just like me" whispered Solomon as he snapped Christian's neck.

Several hours later.

Christian gasped for air as he violently awakens from his slumber, finding himself in someone's bedroom instead of his usual living quarters in the barn with the rest of the slaves. With further investigation, he realized it wasn't just any bedroom; it was the Master's bedroom. He immediately hopped out the bed so fast he finds himself on the other side of the room. "How in the world did I do that" he thought to himself. He looked down at his body and he was completely healed. No sign of him being whipped or being clawed to death by those white devils. He saw a pair of clothes laid out on the end of the bed with a note that said, "For Christian." He examined the clothes and they were much better quality of fabric than he was accustomed to. He took off his blood-stained work clothes and put on the new khaki slacks and white button shirt.

As he was fastening the last buttons on his white collared shirt; a strange aroma lingered up from down stairs. Christian knew it was a familiar scent and that's when he realized what the aroma was. It was the scent of blood calling to him like a beacon gently flickering in the darkness. He couldn't resist any longer, so he descend to the lower part of the house. Once Christian made his way down stairs he found the source of the blood aroma that was calling to him. Scattered in different locations in the living room of this massive plantation home were the lifeless bodies of the Slave masters three daughters. One was slumped over on the couch with puncture marks on her neck. In the corner of the room seated on the floor, head leaning on the wall with similar puncture marks on her neck, was a second daughter. The third and final daughter was being drained of her blood right before Christian's eyes. Solomon was standing in front of the fireplace, still dressed in his black cloak with the Slave Masters daughter in his arms. She hung there in his arms lifeless with her eyes still open staring at Christian.

    Solomon felt Christians presents, so he looked up from his meal, blood dripped from his lips.

    "Christian it's so nice to of you to join us. We are celebrating your new-found freedom, and to celebrate I have a few gifts for you" Solomon points to the dining room. Christian looked in the direction of the dining room. He gasped at what he saw. Hanging from the ceiling by its arms and neck with chains was a beast. Not like the white men he fought previously. It was a wolf the size a man. It had the face and body of a wolf but it stood on its hind legs as it appeared to be unconscious.

"It appears your Master is an alpha werewolf. That's why he looks like a full wolf not like the beta's you encountered in the woods. Now, be cautious my child. Don't get too close, for if he bites you, his venom will kill you and it will be a slow and painful death. Not even my blood can heal you from a wolf's bite" Christian took Solomon's advice keeping his distance. As Christian gazed at the Slave Master with fierce intensity, the beast regains consciousness.

"Look who decided to rejoin the celebration" replied Solomon as he joined Christian in the dining room. The slave master opened his eyes which burned a bright ruby red, staring at Christian. He tried to reach for Christian and Solomon, barking and clawing at them unable to break free from his shackles.

Christian never flinched as he stood in the presence of this monster. Solomon was impressed.

"Before we take care of this monster, there is something you need to do first."

Solomon snapped his fingers and from the kitchen emerged the Slave Masters wife. Christian turned around as she slowly walked towards him. She was dressed in a long white silk nightgown. Several of the buttons were undone revealing the soft snow white flesh of her breast.

"Isn't she the object of your obsession?" Solomon whispered to his son, "Take her my child, and complete your transformation."

The Slave Master's wife was standing in front of Christian awaiting his next move. Christian could hear the sound of her heart beat, the blood coursing through her veins loud and clear. It was like the rushing of the waves heard through a sea shell. She steps in closer to Christian, moving her long auburn hair to expose the soft snow-white flesh of her neck. He licked his lips as the thirst starts to take over. Christian takes the woman into his arms as his breathing becomes heavy. He placed his face against the soft flesh of her neck inhaling her essence deeply. In the background, the chained beast tried with all its might to break free from its chains but was too weak. Christian, unable to fight the thirst any longer sank his fangs into the delicate flesh of the Slave Masters wife. The beast let out a roar that echoes through the walls of the home. Christian drank deep getting his fill. Solomon places his hand on Christian's shoulder.

"That will be enough my son, we still have a need for her." said Solomon calmly. Christian released his grip, letting her limp body hit the floor with a thud.

"You have completed your transition, now you are like me, my son. Now kneel" replied Solomon

Obeying his father's command, Christian kneeled. Solomon opened his cloaked, removing his sword from its sheath. Solomon placed his blade on Christian's shoulder.

"You are now a member of the White Clan. From this day forth you will be known as Christian White, Son of Lord Solomon White. Now rise my son, there is one more thing left for you to do"

Christian stood up as Solomon handed him his sword. "This Sword is made of pure silver. It's the only thing that can kill a werewolf" said Solomon. Christian admire the craftsmanship of the blade, the sword had a gold hilt that was laced with fine brown leather. From the looks of it, you would think it came straight out of medieval times. Christian turned his attention to the beast chained up still snarling at him.

Christian walked up to him, getting as close as he could without being in harm's way. Christian's emerald green eyes stared into the ruby eyes of the beast as it tried desperately to break free. Christian gripped the sword and with all his might swung the blade chopping the beast in half at the waist. The wolf's insides splashed on the hardwood floor as the top half of the werewolf hung by the chains, transforming back into its human form.

"Excellent my son!" boasted Solomon proudly. Solomon walked towards the door, heading outside to stand on the porch, with Christian following behind him. Solomon gazes over the field of crops, lost in thought.

"What now Father?" asked Christian curiously.

"We will need to continue to operate the plantation as normal so we do not draw any unwanted attention from the locals. We will run things from the shadows and grow our numbers. We will use the woman to be our eyes and ears during the day since we cannot walk during the daylight."

"Tomorrow evening I want you go to the other slaves and select just a few that I shall offer the gift to. If any refuse just simply compel them to forget."

"Compel?" asked Christian.

Solomon smiles, "Yes my child. I will teach you this technique and many others in due time. For now, let's heal our hostess so she can tidy up the place. We have much to discuss"

PRESENT DAY

Raven has finally stopped crying and is now taking notice of her new surroundings, still unsure how she even got there in the first place. Alex is standing next to the mini bar pouring cognac into crystal glasses. He brings one to Raven, who was admiring the artwork hanging on the wall. "Here you go", said Alex as he hands her the crystal glass of cognac. "Thank you" she replied as she continued looking at the many pieces of artwork on the wall.

"Your home is beautiful, it's very Victorian."

"Thank you, it was built back in the early 1900's. I've had something's updated throughout the centuries, buts it's all original."

"The 1900's? How old are you?"

"Well, I was twenty-five years old before I was turned into this, 150yrs ago."

"What do you mean before you were turned into this?"

"Originally I was born a Werewolf. My family was a pack of wolves, guardians to a royal family of Vampires who lived in this home."

"You're kidding, right??"

"Let me show you" Alex sits his drink down. Taking Raven by the hand, leading her down a long hallway. On the walls were hand painted portraits of men and woman. Each portrait had a name plate under them with their name and the year.

"Who are these people on the wall" asked Raven curiously.

"These are the past Alpha wolves of my pack. The portraits date back as far as Egyptian times. Werewolves aren't immortal like vampires. We age but at an extremely slow rate. The oldest member of our pack was 700 years old before"

"Before what?"

'Don't worry about it; I'll save that story for another day."

They arrive in the main living room. The room was decorated in the same Old Victorian style. Over the fireplace was a portrait of a beautiful black woman sitting on a throne dressed in a gorgeous royal blue gown and long white hand gloves. Resting on her head was a crystal tiara that was filled with diamonds. Even in this portrait the diamonds twinkled like stars in the evening sky. Standing next to her, dressed in something similar to a military jacket in the same royal blue color as the young woman's gown was Alex. He had on White paints and black riding boots. His jacket was decorated with medals made of gold, and a sword in its sheath sat on his hip.

"Who is that?" asked Raven.

That is Princess Isis, the last female pureblood vampire of her clan. Her clan was hunted down and ran out of Egypt by a Roman hunter who wanted immortality. Her family stayed behind along with my pack, giving her time to escape. I was only a pup at the time.

"Wow that's horrible. But if she escaped then what happened to her.?"

Alex doesn't say anything for a moment as he stares at the portrait lost in thought. In a gentle almost sad voice he replies, "It's a long story…."

Raven takes a seat in a nearby chair, "Well I'm not going anywhere so tell me."

Alex contemplates for a moment. "If we are going to be working together I guess you should know what you have gotten yourself into. It all started back in 1865 in the great state of Georgia…."

GEORGIA 1865

Twenty years have passed since Solomon arrived on the Plantation. He continued running the Plantation as normal until recently an amendment was passed giving all slaves their freedom. Many of the slaves have left the plantation heading up north to start their new lives as free men and women. White people were still having a difficult time accepting black men and women as equals. As some slaves traveled in search of a new home they were met with resistance from white men donning white sheets and pointed hoods which hid their identity. These men were ruthless. They traveled in large groups that were coined lynch mobs. They would harass blacks, scaring them, and trying to force them out of their neighborhoods. They would leave burning crosses in black folk's yards, and in some cases, black men and women were met with violence. Black people were being beaten, burned and hung from trees, left on display as a warning to others. With all this going on outside of the plantation gates, most of slaves stayed to live on the plantation. Those who stayed were given the gift of immortality and now worked for Lord Solomon and his now six sons.

  One night these white men dressed in their white robes caught word of a black men running a plantation where white men worked in the fields. Outraged, these white men gathered their numbers to take visit to this plantation. Riding horses, carrying torches and various weapons; fifteen white sheets made their way down the long dirt road leading to Solomon's plantation home. As they raced towards the home they were met by a young black man standing in the road. The white sheets brought their horses to a halt. The young black men was dressed in black slacks, a white collared shirt and a black vest with a sword in its sheath resting on his hip as he gazed at the white men dressed in their robes with his emerald eyes.

"Boy, you need to move out of our"

"Or what?" replied the young man cutting off one of the white men in mid-sentence.

The group fell silent. "I'll give you all one chance to turn around and never return to my home again."

The men in white robes busted out into hysterical laughter, but the young man didn't crack a smile.

"You are a cocky nigger, aren't you? What's your name boy so we can tell the rest of your people who is responsible for what we are about to do to them" replied the Grand Wizard.

As he pulled his sword from its sheath the young man replied," My name is Christian White and you shall not pass."

The Grand Wizard pulled out a gun from under his white robes then pointed it at Christian, "I guess this is where you die boy."

In the time, it took him to finish his sentence Christian had vanished. Suddenly the sound of one of his men, screaming in agony could be heard behind him. When he turned around one of his men was headless. His lifeless body fell off its horse. The rest of the men started to panic. The flames of their torches started to go out one by one until the men were in complete darkness. The only light they had was from the moon of the evening sky.

    The leader started to lose his cool as the screams of his men filled the air all around him. He could hear the sound of a sharp object cutting through the air as it chopped down his men one by one. Fearing for his life, he started firing his gun blindly into the darkness. He wasn't sure who he was shooting he just wanted to kill the black man. He emptied his six-shot revolver into the darkness. Everything was silent until he heard the sound of a flame being sparked behind him. When he turned around it was Christian standing before him. He was holding his sword down at his side covered in blood in one hand and holding a torch in the other. The Grand Wizard looked around to find the lifeless bodies of his men scattered on the ground. He tried to reload his revolver but his hands were shaking from fear.

    Christian started to walk towards the man. The man started to step backwards as he frantically tries to reload his gun as he trips over one of the bodies of his fellow clansmen. He falls to the ground dropping the bullets to his revolver; the leader starts to beg for his life but Christian ignored his pleads as he walked towards the man. Christian grabs the man by his ankle with such force that he crushes the bones. The man screamed in agony as he was being dragged towards the house. Christian dragged the man behind the home into the woods. The man was now sobbing, begging for his life to be spared, but his cries fell on deaf ears. Christian stopped in front of a large oak tree located deep in the woods behind the home. He released his grip on the man's ankle letting it fall to the ground with a thud. He grabbed some rope that sat up against the tree to make a noose. He pulled the man up by his white robes. The man tried to fight back but he was overpowered by Christian as he wrapped the noose around his neck. He takes the other end of the noose and tosses it over a branch high in the tree. He grabs the other end of the noose and starts to pull the man in the air. The man struggles desperately to avoid being hung but was no match for Christian unnatural strength. The man is now trying to balance on his tippy toes gasping for air. Christian walks over to the man, to whispers in his ear, "This is for my people."

The man tries to speak but the noose around his neck was too tight. Christian pulled on the rope just enough so the man's feet were barely off the ground. In the end, the man died a slow, painful death and from that day forth the plantation was never visited by the white robes again.

With no more interruptions Christians and his brethren were able to complete the task given to them by Solomon. Over the next couple of months Lord Solomon had his people preparing their home for a special guest. From the remodeling, to building of additional rooms; the construction started in the beginning of summer, lasting until the middle of winter two years later, and now the home was finally ready for the arrival of his special guest.

It was a cold winter evening; Lord Solomon paced back and forth in front of the fireplace. "Everything must be perfect my son's our guest arrives tonight", he replied.

Christian stood leaning on the large doorway of the living room watching his father pace. Christian has never seen his father so nervous. Jag was standing by the window gazing out at the dirt road leading to the house. Christians other brothers

Brain, Devin, Michael and Benjamin were all sitting in the living room as well.

"What is so special about this woman? There are plenty women to choose from here in the south" questioned Christian. Solomon stopped pacing, directing his attention to Christian. "She is very special my son. She is the last surviving pure blood vampire of noble blood"

"And that means what exactly?" replied Jag not taking his eyes from the window.

"Only pure blood vampires can create vampire children and with her being of noble blood, it will make us royalty as well"

From the shadows emerged a horse drawn carriage, as it made its approach down the gravel road. "It looks like we'll finally get to meet her" replied Jag.

Without hesitation, everyone rose from their seats, rushing for the porch. Solomon and his six sons stood on the porch eagerly watching the one horse drawn carriage slowly make its way down the dirt road. The carriage was luxurious. It was made of black oak wood, with golden accents on the doors handles, windows, and along the top of the carriage where additional luggage could be stored. The windows were draped with thick cotton and satin red curtains used to keep out the sunlight during daytime travel. The carriage stopped in front of the house just a few feet away from the steps. The driver of the carriage hopped down from his seat. He wasn't dressed like a southern gentleman like Solomon and his sons. He was dressed more like the rugged men of the west, with his brown hat low concealing most of his face. He wore a poncho that looked hand made by Native Americans, khaki pants and brown boots. Around his waist was a gun holster filled with regular bullets, wooden bullets and a chrome revolver with a pearl handle.

He walked back to the door of the carriage cautiously checking his surroundings before opening the carriages door. Solomon and his sons watched as the suspense built up as they anticipated seeing the princess. The driver opened the door then proceeded to kneel bowing his head as he extending his hand. From the carriage emerged the most beautiful woman that any of the vampires had ever seen. She took the driver's hand as he helped her out of the carriage. Her long, silky, black hair was bone straight as it blew in the wind. Her skin was a golden brown that looked as soft as Egyptian cotton. Her eyes burned a luminous amber color that twinkled as they caught the flicker of a nearby flame of a torch. She wore an all-white gown with a long train covered up by a black crush velvet hooded cape with a black satin bow.

Solomon stood speechless, stunned by her beauty, even Christian couldn't deny she was stunning. Solomon stepped off the porch, down to the carriage to greet his guest. "Welcome to my home. I' am Solomon White; it is truly an honor to finally meet you your highness" said Solomon as he bowed. These are my sons Christian, Jag, Michael, Devin, Benjamin and Brian"

"The pleasure is mine. I'm Princess Isis and this is my royal guard Alexander" replied the princess in a soft angelic voice.

"Oh, so he is a werewolf? I wasn't aware the royal guard still existed. So that makes him a member of the Knight pack" replied Solomon intrigued.

"Yes, like me, he is the last of his pack as well as an Alpha no less" smiled the princess.

"I see, well he is welcomed to our home as well"

Christian and his brethren looked at Alex with disgust when they heard what he was.

"Father you aren't seriously allowing this mutt into our home?" snapped Christian

Alex tipped his hat up from his face, glaring at Christian with eyes burning ruby red with a gaze that could strike fear in the hearts of men. "You want to say that again" replied Alex in a low sinister tone as he reached for the chrome revolver on his hip.

"Oh, look, the dog speaks" smiled Christian as his brother's laugh.

"Christian, hold your tongue!" demanded Solomon.

The princess placed her hand on Alex's shoulder to calm him as she addresses Solomon, "I won't tolerate your sons disrespect towards me or my guardian"

"Please forgive my son's outburst. He has had a horrible experience with werewolves in the area. Let's all relax and go inside, dinner is almost ready"

Isis agreed, and then followed Solomon into his home. Alex gathers the princess's luggage before following her into the home.

Inside the home the servants were preparing the long table for dinner for two. The table was decorated with the finest china, silver utensils and candle holders. Solomon and Isis were already seated at the table. Standing behind Solomon to his right was Christian as he watched Alex take his place behind Isis standing to her right.

"So how did you escape Egypt?" asked Solomon as his servants poured blood into his glass.

"While the Roman hunters were purging the city, my father the king put me and Alex's mother on a boat. We watched as my kingdom burned while we drifted down the Nile. We sailed until we ended up off the coast of Italy"

"I see, well you are home now and together we will build a vampire nation here in America"

"A Vampire Nation? What about the other supernatural beings?" asked Isis.

"My only concern is our kind, no offense Alex. You see witches have their coven, werewolves have their packs, and even humans have their hunter guilds. Vampires are the only ones without any kind of unity, besides the individual clans of old. That's why I want to create that for our kind"

"Hmm, that's very ambitious, how do you plan on getting the other clans to agree to this?"

"I just want what's best for our kind. We can continue this conversation later. For now, let's retire for the evening, the sun will be rising soon. Alex, you are free to stay in one of the rooms in house"

"Thank you, sir, But I'll be fine sleeping in the carriage"

"Where you belong" mumbled Christian.

"You would do your best to mind your manners young one" replied Isis sternly

"Christian you are dismissed" snarled Solomon.

Christian bowed before exiting the dining room. As he was leaving Alex took his two fingers and made the walking gesture while they exchanged evil looks.

"Alex, you may retire as well, I'll be fine" said Isis. Alex bowed, "Yes, your majesty" he replied as he made his way outside

After being dismissed by my mistress, I made my way down the porch stairs towards our carriage. It's been a long journey traveling from the western part of the country. I rubbed my horse on her neck as I passed to climb up into my seat on the carriage. I pulled on the reins to signal my horse it was time to go. Like a noble steed she obeyed. I found a nice quiet place in the woods to park the carriage to make camp. Strolling through the woods looking for firewood, I couldn't help but think about the princess and this arranged marriage. I didn't like it not one bit. This Solomon was nothing more than a common vampire. Sure, he was a blue blood; which was another term used for someone born vampire, but he was no noble. Ever since the purge of Egypt, blue bloods have become nothing more than endangered species, living in the shadows ,turning humans to replenish their numbers. Ugh, the thought of him touching her infuriated me. What am I saying!

She is a vampire, a noble and I'm nothing more than a servant we could never be.

I found the last few pieces of wood needed to create a fire, so I started to head back to the carriage. After cooking a rabbit, I caught on the way here; I put the fire out, because I was ready to turn in for the night. I slept in the carriage; it was too cold to be sleeping outside on the ground. I laid there in silence, staring at the ceiling for what felt like hours. I tossed and turned all night, I just couldn't get comfortable. When I finally found a semi comfortable position, there was a gentle tap at the carriage door. I jumped up reaching for my revolver until I noticed the sweet scent of honey and lavender; I knew it could be only one person. When the door opened, it was Princess Isis. She had on a black crushed velvet cape with a little satin bow. She entered the carriage, closing the door behind her. With one hand, she pushed me down on to the floor as she climbed on top of me. She caressed my lips with her finger while her other hand ran gently across my chest. Taking her sharp fingernails, she applied just enough pressure to draw blood. I let out a soft moan from the pain but she shushed me and like an obedient servant I obeyed. Blood trickled from my wounds that healed as fast as she made them.

The sight of my blood aroused her. Her eyes began to glow like soft candle light as she bit her bottom lip. Unable to resist the urge she slowly licked the blood from my chest. It took everything inside me to fight the urge to moan.

She kissed me from my chest traveling up my neck to my lips. She bit my bottom lip drawing more blood. I growled softly as I flipped her over onto her back. My eyes burned ruby red and my breathing was heavy. We were chest to chest as I ran my lips against her neck, her scent was intoxicating. I could feel her body shiver as she felt my breath on her. From here you can just use your imagination. Once we were done exploring each other. We laid there in silence, her head on my chest as I ran my fingers through her black silky hair. Suddenly she slowly sat up. I laid there watching as she fixed her hair, and then put her black satin cape back on. She looked back at me smiling. She winked at me and like that she was gone, vanished. Even though I've seen her teleport many times before it's still amazing. Too bad werewolves don't evolve and get abilities like that. I would love to be able to teleport like her.

For the next few weeks this is how we spent our early morning. During the evening Solomon and the princess spent most of their time together planning the wedding and the proposal for Solomon's "Vampire Nation". The wedding guest list only included the last three remaining noble vampire clans. They were needed to witness their union to make it official. Tomorrow was the big night and just like clockwork Princess Isis appeared at the carriage. Tonight, was different instead of making love we just laid together, enjoying the little time we had together, because after tonight she will belong to Solomon. As I caress her back I say to her, "Tomorrow is the big day."

She softly sighs, "Let's not talk about that, I just want to enjoy this moment. It can very well be our last my love. As we kissed I started to pick up the scent that could only be described as the scent of death and it was surrounding us. I whispered in the princess's ear, "I think we have company." She rushed to gather her things as I went outside to see who our guest were. Standing outside the carriage, twenty vampires emerged from the shadows surrounding the carriage. Among them were Solomon's sons.

"Lord Solomon is very displeased with you you're majesty, we know you are there, come on out and join us" replied

Christian. Moments later Princess Isis exited the carriage, taking her place behind me.

"For the past week's Princess, I've been keeping my eye on you and your guard dog. Personally, I didn't trust a werewolf on our land, but what I didn't expect was to see you and this filthy beast being intimate. I immediately informed Lord Solomon but he was too naïve to believe me. He said I needed proof. So what better way to get proof than having all of us, witnessing you here tonight?"

As Christian gave his diabolical villain speech, I surveyed the area. The only way we were getting out of this was if we fought our way out.

I whispered to the princess," Do you remember what I've taught you? She replied, "Yes my Love."

Christian signals his small army of followers to attack. Princess Isis kicked the bottom of the carriage which opened a secret compartment. She reaches in the compartment pulling out the sword that was being concealed there. I transform into my first formation. In this form, I still resemble a human but with slight animal features. My ears are pointed, my fangs and claws are longer and of course my eyes burned ruby red, the mark of an Alpha. The princess and I stood back to back before engaging in combat.

The princess moved with a quickness that is almost unseen to the naked eye. She sliced and stabbed through vampires one after another in one fluid motion. I was a spectator for brief moment. To see Isis in combat was a very rare treat. I watched for a moment longer. Not wanting to be left out of the fun, I charged three vampires who were approaching. I clawed them down instantly. These vampires were no match for us. With the princess being over several thousand years older than any of these vampires, she overpowered them easily.

Christian and his brothers stood by watching their men being slaughtered by the Princess and I. realizing they may have underestimated their opponents, they crept back into the darkness. The princess saw this and yelled to me, "Go after them, and don't let them get reinforcements!" Without hesitation I gave chase. Two vampires tried to block me from following their leader. I plowed through them like scissors in a wet paper bag, clawing through their flesh as I zoomed past. I moved swiftly through the woods as I perused Christian and the others. I know they couldn't have gotten far so they must be lurking in the shadows trying to ambush me. I came to a clearance in the woods where I started to pick up their scent. I stopped to check my surrounding. Their vampire stench was getting stronger; suddenly they emerged from the shadows. Christian and his five brothers had me completely surrounded. "Six against one, I like these odds," I replied grinning from ear to ear.

"Let's see if you still grinning after we take your life mutt" snarled Christian. Without warning they attacked me all at once. They were quicker than I expected, I was able to react quickly but not fast enough to block all of their attacks. If I blocked a punch from Christian that left me open for an attack from one of his brothers. It was like I was in the eye of a tornado as they circled around me punching, clawing and kicking me. All I could do was cover my face, protecting myself as much as I could until I could react. The barrage of attacks felt like it would never end and that's when I noticed my opportunity. One of the brothers who I believed was named Devin, had to slow down to attack. His punches were coming in wide leaving himself open. This was what I was waiting for. I kept my eye focused on Devin until he was positioned in front of me. I kept my face covered until the last possible moment. He threw his punch wide just as I expected leaving his chest exposed. I made my move; I leaped towards him plunging my clawed hand into his chest, tackling him to the ground. Before he could get a word out I ripped his heart from his chest. The others were still running in a circle before they even realized what happened. When they final stopped, they found me standing over top of their brother.

The sight of seeing their brother lying on the ground lifeless left them temporarily stunned as the horrifying image was being burned into their memory I shouted, "Hey catch!" I smiled, tossing the heart into Michael's hands. Filled with rage, Michael screamed as he charged me. "No wait!" shouted Christian but his words fell on deaf ears. Anger had consumed Michael; he wanted nothing more than to avenge his fallen brother. Michael was swinging at me trying desperately to land a punch but I evaded his attacks effortlessly. He was no match for me one on one. My many years of hand to hand combat training had made me a deadly weapon. Growing bored with my opponent, when he threw his next punch I caught it, using his own momentum against him, I spun him around into a vicious choke hold that placed me standing behind him pinning one of his arms behind his back. I wrap my other arm around his neck capturing his throat in between my bicep. Christian, Jag, Ben and Brian charged me to save their brother but it was already too late. I bit Michael on his shoulder. His cold blood gushed from the wound. I released my grip and kicked Michael in the back sending him flying into Christian and the others. They caught him but the force sent the group crashing into the ground.

I let out roar that could be heard high into the heavens as the blood of my victim covered my face, slowly trickling down my chin. Christian and the others tried to help Michael on his feet as he started to experience the side effects of my bite. Werewolf venom is deadly to vampires, from the wound you could see light blue veins extending from the bite marks, traveling down his shoulder to the rest of his body. At this moment Christian and the others looked at me and on their faces, you could see the look of defeat. They knew this is where they would die.

Slowly I walked towards them, I growled letting them know the inevitable was near. I stood just inches away from them when suddenly I felt a sharp pain in my chest as I started to spit up blood. When I looked down at my chest, a silver blade was protruding through my chest cavity as I was being lifted up off the ground. I was suspended in the air for a brief moment before being tossed to the side like a rag doll. I hit the ground hard dislocating my shoulder as I rolled and tumbled. Standing in front of Christian and the others was Lord Solomon holding his silver sword at his side.

"Get off the ground and grab you brother, we're leaving" barked Solomon. He walked over to me and snatched me off the ground by my shirt collar. "Don't worry I'll take good care of the princess" snarled Solomon. Looking him in his amber glowing eyes I replied, "Go to hell," as I spit blood in his face. Solomon choke slammed me into the ground making a small creator then kicked me in the gut knocking me unconscious.

Lying on the ground in a puddle of my own blood I felt someone shaking me. When I opened my eyes, I found myself lying in the arms of the princess.

"Speak to me Alex! Don't you die on me! Why aren't you healing" she said frantically as tears run down her face.

"Solomon stabbed me with a blade made of silver. I don't think I'm going to make it"

"I'm not going to let you die on me!" The princess bit deep into her wrist drawing her blue blood. "Here drink" she replied desperately.

"Now you know that will not work on me. Drinking your blood could kill me"

"You're dying anyway damn it, I order you to drink my blood!"

She puts her wrist to my lips and I dank deeply, consuming a large quantity of her blood. I can feel the wound in my chest begin to heal when suddenly my body starts to reject her blood. I went into shock, shaking and foaming a blue froth from my mouth.

"No, no, no Alex!" screamed the princess as I lay dying in her arms. Suddenly the princess is pulled from the ground. I try desperately to hold on to her but my grip was too weak. It was Solomon pulling the Princess away from me. I reached out tugging on his leg trying to stop him but three loud bangs rang out. When I looked up Solomon was pointing a gun at me. He had shot me three times in the chest. I gasp for air as the silver bullets pierce through my chest. I released my grip on his leg as I felt the clutches of death pulling me away. Taking my final breath, the last thing I saw before falling into the darkness of the abyss was Christian running his sword through the princess, ending her life.

"Wake up Alex, It's not your time yet" whispered the Princesses voice as it snatches my consciousness back from death's cold grip. I sprung up as if I was awaking from a horrible dream letting out a roar that didn't sound like my own. I was breathing heavily as I placed my hand on my chest. The wounds from the sword and gun shots had completely healed, which was odd because wounds created by silver stops a werewolf's healing ability making him heal at the rate of a normal human. I was still trying to understand what was going and that's when I saw it.

Lying just a few feet away from where I sat was the Princess. I felt my heart sink to the pit of my stomach as I started to panic.

"No, no, no, not my baby" I thought to myself as I crawled over to her. I held her lifeless body tightly in my arms, rocking back and forth begging her to wake up, just open your eyes, but I knew she was gone. It felt like a part of me had truly died. This was the worse pain I've ever felt; no physical pain could compare. Tears rolled down my face as the realization that my one true love had been taking from me. For the first time in my life I felt lost, she was my world and now that world was gone. Creeping over the horizon was her mortal enemy, the sun. I only had a few moments left to mourn her before she was no more. As the sun slowly took its place in the sky, Isis began to turn into ashes in my arms until she was nothing more than dust being carried away by the wind.

Filled with rage I let out a roar that shook the heavens. I could feel pain, anger, grief and despair bubbling inside me like a boiling pot of hatred. All I could think of was killing Solomon, Christian and the rest of his brothers. I let it consume me, allowing it to transform me. This feeling was different, I felt a power I've never felt before, I felt invincible and I liked it. I felt me shifting into my full werewolf form but something was different.

My skin turned a greyish black as the fur emerged traveling up my arm and all over my body leaving only my abdominal and chest bare, with the new greyish black flesh. "What is this," I thought to myself. I was half man, half beast. Before I could fully examine my new form, the thirst hit me and in an instant, I vanished.

The next thing I remember is waking up on the living room floor of Solomon's plantation home covered in blood with corpses scattered all over the house.

It was still daylight outside so I knew Solomon and the others were not among the corpses that filled the house. With no clue where they could be I set the house with all the bodies of the servants inside on fire along with all the crops outside leaving no trace of them or me to be found.

PRESENT DAY

Raven was curled up on the couch with tears in her eyes.

"After that, I spent the next one hundred and fifty years traveling the world following every lead, every whisper anything that remotely sounded like Christian or his brothers. Which brings us to now" replied Alex.

Wiping her tears, "So that's why you were at the party, to kill Jag?"

"Yes, but I didn't expect to meet you"

"So, now what?"

"Now, I train you, as your Alpha it's my responsibility to teach and nurture you in our ways. When I'm done with you, you will be able to get your revenge and kill a few vampires along the way"

"So, when do we start?" asked Raven

"We will start in the morning, for now let me show you to your room"

EPISODE 5

"EVE UNDER THE SUN"

Standing in the center of a training mat, shirtless, barefoot wearing a pair black hakamas was Christian White. The dojo was filled with the soft light of a thousand candles as Christian performed his intense training regimen. He stood in his fighting stance, motionless like a mannequin. His feet were a little more than shoulder width apart with a slight bend in his knees. He fully extended his right arm out to his side with his head looking in the same direction. In his left hand he held a katana; its blade was made of pure silver. Similar to Solomon's medieval saber, but instead Christian went with the way of the samurai. After being nearly defeated not once but twice by a werewolf, he thought it would be in his best interest to learn to defend himself. He has had more than hundred years to perfect his technique making him deadly with the katana.

He slowly raised the katana in the air, bending his elbow so that the blade ran parallel over his head with his right arm. He took a deep breath, and then proceeded with his training. He moved smoothly as he carefully guided his blade through a variety of sequences as he slashed, feinted and thrust at his imaginary opponent. Christian picked up the pace, moving his silver blade at blinding speed making it appear as nothing more than a soft white light cutting through the air.

As he continued his training, an unexpected visitor entered the dojo. Christian didn't stop his training; he simply ignored his unwanted visitor who now stood at the edge of the training mat.

"I need your help" said Jag as he watches Christian train.

"Well if it isn't Solomon's new favorite. What's so important that brings you all the way down here where us lower class vampires dwell?" replied Christian without missing a beat as he went from sequence to sequence with his silver katana.

"There has been a situation in the District that needs your expertise"

Christian propelled himself into the air twisting and twirling his body like an Olympic gymnast landing a few feet from where Jag stood. Using that momentum, twirling his blade over his head and around his body in a blur of soft white light bring the tip of his blade just inches from Jags throat. Jag didn't flinch as they stared at each other like two gunslingers at high noon.

"So, what's this situation" asked Christian, still pointing his blade at Jags throat.

Jag raised his right hand using two fingers he slowly moved the blade from his neck, "Let me start from the beginning"

Twenty-four hours earlier

Empty blood bags cover the kitchen floor of Jags luxurious home. The refrigerator was open as an unconscious Eve sat on the floor, slumped over up against the kitchen cabinets. In her hand was an empty wine bottle of blood. Regaining consciousness, she rubbed her forehead like she was recovering from a hangover. She raised the bottle to her mouth only to find it empty. She reached for the blood bags on the floor around her to find them empty as well, even the refrigerator was empty. She sluggishly picked herself off the floor using the island to pull herself on her feet.

She frantically checked every cabinet; closet and the pantry only to find that she had completely went through Jags entire blood supply. The thirst was growing inside her; it felt as if she had been stranded on a deserted island with nothing to drink for weeks and she needed to satisfy this craving immediately. She went to the living room and flopped down on the couch. She placed her face in her hands stressing herself about how she was going to get more blood. Mauling over different ideas, she heard the sound of a car pulling up. She ran to the window like a little puppy hoping it was Jag returning home. She threw open the curtains only to find it wasn't him, instead it was the neighbor who lived across the street. She pouted when realizing it wasn't who she expected. She stayed in the window watching as her neighbor got out his car.

He was a young man who looking like he was in his early twenties. He was brown skin with curly black hair and a slender build. It's hard to really tell how old he is seeing that vampires are immortals that don't age. Eve continued watching the young man as he moved to the trunk of the car. He opened the trunk, pulling out a large white box with a red cross on the front of it. Eve's eyes lit up with excitement because she knew what was inside the white box. She finally had an idea, she decided to go over to introduce herself to her new neighbor and ask to borrower some blood.

She knew how ridiculous that sound but she didn't have any other option. The thirst was getting worse, causing her severe abdominal pains. With her mind made up she proceeded with her plan. The neighbor was already in his home before Eve could get out the house. She quickly crosses the street. Anxious to get herself a blood fix, she knocked on the door as if she was the police.

The neighbor opens the door with a look of confusion on his face. He looks Eve up and down, sizing her up, "Can I help you" replied the man.

"Hi, I just moved in across the street, my name is Evelyn, pleased to meet you" said Eve with a smiled as she extending her hand to greet her new neighbor. The man was hesitant, wondering what this strange woman was doing at his door.

"I know this may sound crazy, but I was hoping you could spare a blood bag or two"

The neighbor took a slight step out his doorway to see if anyone else was around, "Is this a joke? I can't help you with that" replied the man as he stepped back into his home. Eve places her hand on the door stopping the man from closing the door on her. She was struggling to keep her composer, cracking the fakest smile she could muster. "I know you can spare at least one blood pack, I just watched you bring a big ass thing of blood in here" Eve replied.

"I don't know who you are lady, but like I said I can't help you, I ain't got anything for you" replied the neighbor as he tried to close the door once again.

Eve could no longer keep her composer; the thirst had taken over. Her eyes began to glow their luminous emerald green as she gazed upon the neighbor with a sinister look. She pushes the door open with such force it sent the man stumbling back into the house. Before the man could regain his footing, Eve was already on the man. She punched the man in the chest with such force the impact sent the man hurling through the air, crashing into the wall and falling to the floor.

Clearing the distance between her and the neighbor in an instance with her super human speed, she was now standing over him. The man wasn't even on his feet when Eve grabbed him by the neck off the ground, hoisting him in the air by his neck.

"Where is it? Where did you put it?" replied Eve with a crazed look in her eye.

"I ain't telling you shit crazy bitch" replied the man as he struggled to speak. He tried to shout for help, and it made Eve extremely annoyed. She worried that someone would hear his cries for help since vampires had superior hearing compared to humans. Eve did the only thing she could do to silence the man. She took her free hand and forced it through his chest ripping out his heart. It happened so quickly that the man had time to see his beating heart in Eve's hands as the light left his eyes.

Eve released her grip on the man letting his lifeless body collapse on the hardwood floor. She tossed his heart at him as she proceeded to search the home for the white container. Her first stop was the kitchen. She went through the refrigerator, every cabinet and closet like a police officer raiding a home, yet she didn't find what she was looking for. She noticed a door slightly open in the hallway. When she opened the door, she found a staircase that lead downstairs possibly to the basement. She flicked the light switch and made her way down stairs.

Once in the basement Eve couldn't believe her eyes. The man's basement looked like it belonged to a museum. There were tons of antique items, from furniture, portraits and pottery. Some of the antiques looked dated no least than a hundred years. The item that caught Eve's attention the most was a rack of ten antique swords. One sword in particular was intriguing to her. Its hilt was made of gold with the head of a wolf at the end. The eyes of the wolf head hilt were made of two tiny red stones. As she admired the blade she couldn't help but feel as if it was calling to her. She couldn't make out what it was saying but it was like a whisper calling to her, the closer she got the louder the whispers. She was standing right in front of the sword rack, moments from grabbing the sword when she noticed the white container with a red cross on it out the corner of her eye. The sight of the container snapped her out her trance.

She rushed over to the container which was sitting on top of the dryer. Eve snatches the top off the container to expose its contents. Inside was twenty blood packs, her eyes light up like a kid in a candy store at the sight. Without hesitation, she grabbed a blood pack ripping the seal off and squeezing the blood out of the packing into her mouth like a juice box. The blood danced on her taste buds as it satisfied the thirst. She couldn't describe the feeling she was experiencing, all she knew it was euphoric. She finishes that blood bag and goes for another. She grabbed the container off the dryer and sat it on the floor. She sat down on the floor next to it, resting her back against the dryer. Taking another blood bag out of the container, she continues to quench her thirst.

Passed out on the basement floor of the neighbor's home, Eve had consumed all of the man's blood supply. The blood had this strange effect on her, like how too much alcohol would affect a human. Eve is suddenly jolted out of her drunken slumber by the horrified screams of a woman. Eve jumped up to find herself still inside the neighbor's home. Eve begins to panic as she hears a woman's voice coming from upstairs. "It must be the man's wife or girlfriend who just found his dead body upstairs" Eve thought to herself. She tries to quietly find a way out of the man's basement but there were no doors or windows. The only way out was to go up the stairs.

Eve begins to panic as she paced back and forth, desperately searching for a way out of the basement. At the top of the basement stairs, Eve could hear the woman on her phone talking to the authorities. Desperation started to set in, Eve didn't want to go to jail for murder or even worse. Eve slowly backed away from the stairs; she was so consumed by the fearing of being captured, she wasn't paying attention to what was behind her as she backed into the antique weapon rack, knocking it over sending the swords crashing to the floor.

Eve put her hands over her mouth, hoping the woman upstairs didn't hear it. But this was not the case. The sound of the woman's footsteps could be heard as she walked to the basement door. She opened the door shouting, "I know you're down there you monster! I called the local guild on your ass! They're on their way you piece of shit"

"This is it" Eve thought to herself. How was she going to get out of this house, she wasn't ready for jail or worse death.

Her mind was racing, as fear of the inevitable started to set in, and then she heard it again, the whispering. She looked around the room with her eyes but saw no one. Lying at her feet was the sword with the golden wolf head. "Is that what's been calling to me?" she thought to herself. She kneeled down to pick up the blade. As soon as Eve placed her hands on the sword the whispering stopped. She removed the sword from its sheath; its blade had a dull matte look to it. She reached out to run her hand across the blade to see if it was sharp but stopped when she heard an ominous, animal like voice in her heard, "Kill her, it's the only way out is through her"

The voice startled Eve, making her drop the sword as it hit the floor with a clang. The woman upstairs continued to scream at Eve from upstairs. With no other options, Eve decided to listen to the voice she heard. She grabbed the sword again and the voice returned. Eve took a deep breath as she gripped the golden hilt of the sword tightly. She didn't want to kill this woman but didn't want to get captured either. "Fuck it" she whispered as she slowly marched up the stairs. Her heart was racing with every step. The woman saw Eve coming up the stairs as they made eye contact. The woman noticed the weapon in Eve's hand. Fearing for her life she ran for the door. Eve knew it was now or never. Using her new found super speed she caught the woman right before she could get to the door. Eve grabbed her by the back of her head. With a fistful of hair, Eve yanked the woman away from the door. Before the woman could scream for help Eve plunged her blade into the woman's abdomen. The woman gasped, unable to scream as the sword pierced her flesh. Eve slid her blade out of the woman as she released her grip on the woman's hair letting her body collapse to the floor.

Eve didn't stay long enough to watch the body hit the floor as she rushed out of the home sprinting over to Jag's house. She rushed into the kitchen towards the garage door snatching a pair of keys that were hanging from a hook on the wall. Eve jumped into Jags spare car, throwing her sword in the back seat. The tires screeched as she reverses the car out the garage. She didn't know where she was going to go all she knew was she had to get out of the District.

Back at the dojo, Christian rubbed his temple as he listened to Jags tale. "Women are going to be the death of you" Mumbled Christian.

"I have men cleaning up the mess now, but we are unable to find her, and that's where you come in" said Jag

"At least you were smart enough to clean up after yourself"

"I'm not incompetent", snarled Jag.

Christian chuckled, "Ok, I'll help you, just go back to the district just in case she returns"

"What are you going to do?"

"I'll take care of it. Do you have a picture of this psycho?" asked Christian.

Jag pulls out his phone to found a suitable picture then sends it to Christian's phone. Christian makes his way to his training bag. He puts his katana in its sheath, laying it up against the bench where his bag sat. He pulled his phone out of the bag to open the text sent by Jag. "Nice, you always knew how to pick the pretty ones." Christian put his phone back in his bag. He placed his bag over his shoulder, picked up his katana then headed for the door in the opposite direction that Jag entered.

"You not gonna hurt her, are you?" replied Jag trying to sound concerned.

Christian didn't turn to look back at Jag as he exited the room, "I told you I'll handle it" replied Christian all nonchalant as he entered locker room of the dojo, away from Jag. He sits his bag on the floor, resting his katana on top of the bag. He grabbed his phone out the bag to look at Eve's picture. "Why the cute one always have to be crazy" he thought to himself as he smiled at the picture. Once he had her image in his head he put the phone down. He sat on the ground with his legs crossed. Placing his fist together like he was giving himself a fist bump, he took a deep breath then closed his eyes.

For the past few months Christian has been having visions, glimpses into the future. At first, he thought they were just another case of Déjà vu. Then he started knowing things before they happen. He knew what was going on. He was evolving. He remembered from the stories Solomon would tell of how pure bloods would gain special abilities through what he called evolution, and only pure bloods possessed this ability. "But if this was the case, then how do you explain what was happening to me" Christian thought to himself.

He cleared his mind of all thought, only focusing on Eve's face. Christian was able to pinpoint the exact location of most vampires who were linked to Solomon's bloodline, whether turned by him or another of his bloodline. As individuals popped up in his mind like hotspots on a map, similar to Professor X using Cerebro, Christian finally found who he was looking for. When he opened his eyes, they were shining their emerald color "I found you!" he said to himself.

Sitting alone at the bar drinking herself into oblivion, Eve contemplated the events that occurred several hours ago in the vampire district. As she took another sip of her cognac something dawned on her. She wasn't really afraid she had killed not one but two people, she was more afraid that she was almost caught and now on the run. Now that she thought about it she didn't have any remorse about it at all. With this new revelation she thought to herself, "Am I monster?" as she finished the last of her drink. Suddenly another thought crossed her mind "What was up with that sword and that......"

Her thought was interrupted by the sound of an unfamiliar voice. Standing beside her was a man. He looked like he was in his early 30's brown skinned, nicely groomed and casually dressed.

"What's a pretty thing like you doing sitting alone at the bar?" said the gentleman.

Eve didn't respond. She frowned, rolling her eyes at him with a look of disgust, turning her attention to the bartender signaling him so she can order another drink.

"Oh, you're the feisty type, I like it" replied the man. The bartender brought Eve another drink and the man paid for it. Eve didn't acknowledge the man's kind gesture, she just took the drink.

"So, what's your name gorgeous"?

"Look, I think you should leave me alone before something bad happens to you?

"I'll take my chances; my name is Lamar. Are you gonna tell me your name or are you gonna make me play the guessing game?" Lamar held his hand out, waiting for Eve to shake his hand.

"I'm not in the mood for this" she thought to herself. She decided to entertain this man so he can hurry up and go away. She barely takes his hand to shake it.

"That wasn't so hard was it" replied the man. He begins to have a conversation with Eve but she is unable to concentrate because the thirst has returned.

"Oh, not right now" she thought to herself. The sound of his blood rushing through his veins was like the sound of waves crashing against the shore to Eve's heightened senses. She could no longer hear what Lamar was rambling about, only god knows what he could be saying. All she could focus on was sinking her teeth into the flesh of this annoying man's neck. Unable to resist the urge anymore, she blurts out, "Let's get out of here!"

Lamar was caught off guard by her spontaneous outburst but he was more than ready to leave the commotion of the crowd. Eve takes him by the hand, pulling him away, better yet dragging him to the back of the club towards the bathrooms.

She forces Lamar into the men's bathroom pushing him into the nearest stall and starts kissing Lamar.

"What's gotten into you? I Like it!" replied Lamar as he tries to take control of the situation. Eve overpowers him, pinning him to the wall with one hand. Lamar is beginning to get slightly worried yet still aroused by her aggressiveness. She ripped his shirt down the middle with her free hand, exposing his bare chest. She kissed him from his neck down to his belly button. Lamar moaned in delight, as Eve's soft lips caress his flesh. She kissed his neck inhaling deeply then exhaling. The warmth of her breath on his neck created goose bumps that traveled down his spine.

With no one around she could finally give into her urges. She grabs Lamar by the head, moving it to the side to expose his neck. "What the ……" before Lamar could finish his sentence, Eve sank her pearly white fangs into Lamar's neck. He screamed in agony, but the loud music of the club drowned out his cries. Eve drank deeply, satisfying her thirst just enough not to kill him. Once she was satisfied, she released her grip on Lamar letting his body fall to the floor. She leaned up against the stall, leaning her head back allowing herself to enjoy the sensation of tasting fresh blood. It was even more pleasurable than she expected.

Lamar struggled to get back on his feet, stumbling out of the stall. "You fucking bitch! You bit me!" shouted Lamar as he tries to staunch the blood flow from his neck with his hand.

Eve looked at Lamar with eyes that glowed green with lust. "Don't worry about that, after I'm done with you, you won't remember a thing"

"What the fuck are you!" replied Lamar with fear in his eyes as Eve slowly walked towards him. He was too weak to run do to the amount of blood loss. Eve grabbed him by the collar pulling him to his feet so she can look him in his eyes. Using a soft, calm voice Eve said to Lamar, "You will forget that any of this has happened. You will forget meeting me here tonight. Go home, get some rest, and when you wake the only thing you will remember is that the bite mark on your neck was made by an animal attack"

Lamar looked at her like she was a complete psycho, "You fucking bit me, How the fuck am I gonna forget that with your crazy ass"

Eve was confused, "Why didn't it work" she said to herself as she released her grip on Lamar. Once he was free from her clutches he seized the opportunity to escape the bathroom. Lamar was about to make his way out the bathroom when someone entered. Lamar was relieved when he saw the man.

"Whooooa, did I come in at a wrong time?" replied the man.

"I gots to get up out of here, that crazy bitch over there just took a bite out my ass!" shouted Lamar.

The man looked over Lamar's shoulder to see Eve sitting on the toilet, confused as if she had a lot on her mind. "Well, don't worry I'll be taking things from here" replied the man to Eve.

"Why you talking to her, I'm the one who is bleeding to death over here! Fuck that crazy……"

The man grabbed the Lamar by the face, covering his mouth with his hand. "Shut up!" replied the man. Lamar instantly fell silent. The man removed his hand from Lamar's mouth. Eve watched, confused by this mysterious man. The man pricked his thumb with his teeth drawing blood. He then rubbed his blood on Lamar's neck healing his bite marks instantly. Eve knew there was no mistake, this man was a vampire.

"Alright now that's taken care of. Now listen very carefully. When you leave this bathroom, you are going to forget ever meet her or me." Lamar nodded in acknowledgment. "Oh, and here get yourself a drink, you've earned it" replied the man as he put twenty dollars in Lamar's hand. Lamar took the money, and then exited the bathroom.

Eve watched slightly terrified, yet intrigued, as the tall stranger, clearly a vampire just rescued her from being discovered. "But why was he here" she thought to herself and at that moment everything became clear. Her worst fear has come to reality.

"Well, well, well this is a fine mess you've gotten yourself into", replied the man. "Oh, I'm sorry, where are my manners? My name is Christian White and it's a pleasure to meet you. You're Eve, right?"

Eve shook her head yes afraid to speak. Christian moved closer to Eve so that he was standing directly in front of her blocking her from escaping.

"I know you have a lot of questions so let me answer a few for you, yes I am a vampire, and yes Jag sent me to deal with you"

"Please don't kill me, I'm not ready to die" pleaded Eve as tears formed in her eyes.

"Save the water works it's not going to work on me. You've killed two vampires by yourself, that's pretty impressive, but the District has a strict policy on violence in the safe zone. So, unfortunately, I can't let you leave here alive."

Eve's heart was racing as the thought of her death crept into her mind. She didn't want to die. "If I'm going to die then I'm going down fighting. I already killed two vampires adding one more won't hurt" she thought to herself. No longer bound by her fear Eve lunged at Christian to rip his heart out like she did her previous victim. But unlike them, Christian was superior to them and her. He pivoted to his right letting Eve's momentum carry her past him. He slapped her on the back with a backhand swing that sent her crashing into the bathroom wall. Eve gasped as the air rushed out of her lungs. Before her feet hit the ground, Christian rushed over to her, palming the back of her head, pinning her to the wall. Christian leaned in so close that she could feel his breath on her neck.

"You're a feisty one aren't you, it would be a shame to kill someone with such potential" Christian whispered in Eve's ear. "I'll give you a choice, I can smash your pretty little head right here and now, or you can come and work for me. I can use someone like you. So, what's it going to be?"

"Did she really have a choice" she thought to herself, as she struggled to break free. "I'll work for you" she shouted.

"Wise decision, now come along" replied Christian releasing his grip on Eve's head. Eve stumbled as her feet touch the floor, rubbing the back of her head, massaging away the pain.

"Where are we going" replied Eve as Christian exited the bathroom ignoring her question. Eve waited a moment wondering what she got herself into, as she followed after Christian. Eve made it outside to find Christian leaning up against an electric blue Porsche 911 GT3 with his arms crossed.

"I don't have all night, sun will be up soon let's go" barked Christian. Eve started towards Christian when the whispering started. "I have to get something out the car" replied Eve.

"Whatever it is, forget it" replied Christian.

Ignoring him, she rushed over to the car she stole from Jag. She opened the back-passenger door and on the back seat sat the sword with the wolf head gold hilt. She grabbed it then rushed back to Christian. He was already sitting in his car tapping his fingers rapidly on the steering wheel. As soon as Eve was in the car Christian put his sports car into first gear, popping the clutch. The force of the takeoff made Eve's head hit the head rest with a thud. The tires screeched like a banshee as the blue sports car zoomed out the parking lot.

"What was so important that you had me waiting? I hate waiting" replied Christian. He looked over at Eve as she was clutching a sword with a gold hilt. "Where did you get that?"

"I found this in that man's basement. It was calling to me" said Eve. Christian couldn't get a good look at the sword, but he had a good idea what she had.

"I think I've made the right choice sparing your life. If I'm not mistaken, that sword you have is a dark object"

"What?"

"It's an object that was created with dark magic that possess special abilities. That one you have there is called 'The Wolf's Fang" I thought it was just a werewolf myth"

"The Wolf's Fang?"

"I don't have all the details but it's said long ago a great werewolf knight was battling an army of vampires but was defeated, left for dead. He was found by a witch who was passing by. He was dying as he begged the witch to spare his life. She asked him what was in it for her... He said he would pledge his allegiance to her, so she agreed. Long story short, unknown to him she had other plans. With a wave of her hand and a sacred incantation, she sealed the werewolf into a sword. That's probably the voice you have been hearing."

"Is that true" she thought to herself as she clinched to the weapon. "So, what is its special power?'

"Well legend says that one cut from this blade will infect its vampire victims with werewolf venom, so I suggest you don't touch its blade."

After a few minutes of speeding through the city, Christian finally made it out of the city limits.

"We're leaving the city? Where are you taking me?" said a concerned Eve.

"Just sit back and ride or I could just pull over and leave you dead in a ditch if you like" replied Christian. Eve wasn't trying to die, so for the rest of the ride Eve sat in silence looking out the window watching the scenery zoom by. Christian maneuvered his sports car through winding back roads like a professional circuit racer. He reached a long strip of road that lead towards a large mountain with no sign of an opening. Instead of slowing down he continued speeding. Eve looked over at the speedometer; the needle was teetering on the one hundred mile an hour mark.

"Are going to slow down?" replied Eve nervously.

Christian didn't respond as he smashed on the clutch, shifting into fifth gear.

"Christian? Christian slow down, that's a fucking mountain! You trying to kill us? CHRISTIAN!" screamed Eve, closing her eyes bracing for impact. Eve sat clinching to her seatbelt. After a few seconds, she opened her eyes to find herself unharmed. She looked over at Christian who had a smirk on his face. "You think that was funny?" replied Eve.

"Where are we? Are we back in the Vampire District?"

"No, this is your new home. I have it hidden by a cloaking spell similar to the one in the District" said Christian. They continued on the long road that leads to a large estate. It was a massive mansion designed in the neoclassical architectural style of the early 1900's. The home was set in the middle of nowhere surrounded by woods with no sign of neighbors for miles. We approached a fountain that stood in the center of the driveway in front of the house. Christian followed the driveway around the fountain and parked the car.

"We're here" said Christian as he exited the vehicle. Eve grabbed her sword, and then followed after Christian.

"Where is here?" asked Eve.

Christian opened the door, gesturing Eve to enter, "Welcome to Shadow Grove, home of The Order of the Black Sun"

Eve walked through the door into the foyer of this beautiful home. Standing next to a larger staircase leading to the upper level of the home was a man with long dreads. His brown skin was covered in tattoos and he had several facial piercings. He stood with his hands behind his back like a solider at attention.

"Welcome home Lord Christian", said the heavily tattooed man"

"Dolla, this is the one we have been looking for. This is Eve and she will be staying with us.

"Wait, what is the order of the black sun?"

"It's an organization of vampires who believe that vampires should rule over all species and not live hidden in the shadows" said Christian. Now Dolla will take good care of you. He will show you the ropes. I'll be back in to check on you periodically. Once you are ready I'll teach you how to use that sword you're so attached to"

"So, you just going to leave me here with this strange man?"

"If you like I can still kill you"

"No, no, no, that's ok…"

"Good, Dolla she is all yours. Make me proud, I have high expectations for you" replied Christian as he exited the home, leaving Eve and Dolla standing in the foyer.

"Well, welcome to the Order of the Black Sun, let's get started" replied Dolla.

EPISODE 6

"KYUKETSUKI TEMPLE"

RAVEN'S POINT OF VIEW

Laying in this massive king size bed, surrounded by fancy black and grey silk pillows, I was awoken by the smell of bacon cooking. I kicked the plush comforter off of me as I jumped out of bed. I grabbed a red terry cloth robe Alex gave me and headed downstairs. In the kitchen Alex was standing at the stove scrambling eggs. He had on his pajama bottoms and a wife beater. The muscles in his back flexed as he sprinkled cheese over the scrambled eggs. The table was covered with food; there were platters of pancakes and French toast sprinkled with powdered sugar, topped with strawberries. He had a variety of fresh fruits and many other things one would eat for breakfast.

"Who is all this food for" I asked, seeing that the large table was only set for two.

"Good morning sleepy head" replied Alex. He came over to the table and pulled my chair out. "I've never had anyone pull my chair out for me" I thought to myself as I sat down. He pushed me up to the table.

"What's the special occasion?" I asked.

"Today is the first day of your training, and the first time anyone, besides myself has occupied this home in over a hundred and fifty years. This breakfast feast is a Knight tradition. A big breakfast to fuel your training."

"Tradition you say?"

"Well of course, you are a Knight now"

The way he looked into my eyes as he called me a Knight made my heart flutter ever so slightly. I know he was just saying I was a part of his pack but it felt like he was saying much more.

He fixed my plate and poured me glasses of orange juice that I'm 100% positive he squeezed himself. I took one bite of my food and it was like my taste buds were in heavenly bliss. The French toast was light and fluffy. The eggs were scrambled to perfection; I could even taste the five different cheeses he used as well.

"Oh my god! Where did you learn how to cook like this?"

"I've had plenty of time to perfect my culinary skills. Now that your senses are on one thousand you can experience things on a whole different level. With a little training, you will learn how to use all your heightened senses to your advantage."

There was enough food to feed a family of at least ten and we finished that gourmet breakfast in record breaking time. I've never ate so much in my life.

"Alright now that's out the way, go upstairs and get dressed we have work to do" replied Alex.

"What about these dishes?" I asked.

He smiled, "Don't worry about it, you go get dressed I'll take care of this"

So, I left him with the dishes as i made my way upstairs. When I got back to my room, I found a pair of orange and a royal blue kimono-like robes and a blue long sleeve under armor shirt. I put on the robes in layers; the blue under armor top fit like it was a second layer of skin, while the robes were more comfortable giving me free range of motion. I caught my reflection in the large mirror that sat in the corner of the room. I looked like a real shaolin monk. I pulled my hair into a ponytail then went back downstairs. When I got downstairs the kitchen was spotless, I looked around like I was in the wrong place. "How did he clean up so fast" I thought to myself. Outside on the patio stood Alex already dressed in the exact same robes, but he wore royal blue and black robes.

I exited the kitchen out onto the patio. I stood next to Alex, from here; there was a great view of the Amalfi Coast. I've never been outside of the United States so this was just a breath-taking view.

"Don't you look cute in your Gee my little apprentice" smirked Alex. "You ready to go"

"Where we going" I asked him curiously.

"You'll see"

Alex took my hand, and then raises his other hand placing his index finger and middle finger on his forehead. In the blink of an eye we were no longer standing in the backyard of the island home, instead we were now standing in the middle of a dirt road. A few feet ahead of us were a black and orange wooden gate that was connected to a wooden bridge. Posted in the ground on each side of the archway were large torches. The bridge was leading into what looked like a small marketplace; at this distance you could hear the hustle and bustle of the crowd as vendors tried to sell their goods.

"I don't think I'll ever get use to that, where are we," I asked.

"We are in a beautiful rural part of Japan" said Alex with a smile. "It's been years since I've been here.

"Why are we in Japan?"

"This is where you will be training. You see that big castle up in the mountains? That's Kyuketsuki temple, that's where we're heading"

"We're staying in a castle! Oh, I've always wanted to see a castle"

"But first we need to make a stop in the village for some supplies"

"So, why did we come all the way to Japan to train? I mean I don't have a problem with it at all. It just seems a little excessive.

"This is where I came to learn control over my new abilities. I wasn't prepared to handle the thirst. So, I came to this place to learn from a great martial arts master who taught me discipline."

We made our way across the wooden bridge that was suspended over a calm flowing river into the village's marketplace. Once we were in the market place you could feel the excitement in the air. The tension was palpable between the merchants and customers as the merchants bartered their goods which varied from exotic foods, clothes, jewelry and even weapons. "This is amazing, it's like being in one of those foreign films" I said as I took in the sights and sounds of the busy market place. As we made our way through the marketplace I began to realize something. I had no idea what they were saying. I don't speak Japanese.

"Alex, you speak Japanese?"

"Well, I spent a good twenty years here so I eventually picked up on it."

Alex continued his negotiations with the merchants as they exchanged dialogue in their native tongue. He purchased a hiking backpack and began to fill it with the different items we acquired as we meandered through the market. After visiting a few more merchants and sampling some of the exotic foods, we were finally ready to make our way up the mountain to Kyuketsuki Temple. At the end of the road was another gate with torches on each side of it. Sitting on a stool next to the archway was an older man wearing a straw hat, smoking a hand rolled cigarette. He wore a chest piece and gauntlets that looked like antique samurai armor and his sword was planted into the ground.

When we reached the gate, the man began to speak earnestly in his native language. I was lost because I had no idea what he was saying, so I turned to Alex, "What is he saying?"

"Raven I would like you to meet a good friend of mine, this is old man Han"

Old man Han stood up and almost stumbled. Then he reached for Raven's hand, but she pulled away from him.

"Is he drunk?"

"Well he may not look it but he is a drunken master so being drunk is like second nature to him. He stands guard at these gates along with his grandson Akio, who clearly wasn't at his post when we entered the village."

"What are the torches for?"

"The locals say there are monsters that feed on the blood of humans living in the bamboo forest. These torches have the magical ability to keep supernatural beings out of the village once they are lit"

"So that's why I seen them throughout the village" said Raven

Alex exchanges dialogue with the man, and then we continued our journey. We entered the bamboo forest, the sun was still high in the sky but I could feel darkness here.

"So, what aren't you telling me Alex, who is the vampire in the castle?" I asked.

Alex didn't look at me, he just continued walking. "It used to be vampires in the temple, but a good friend of mine Tamotsu and I changed all that. He is the last of his clan and has been watching over these lands for many years."

We made our way through the bamboo forest until we reached a set of stone stairs that were carved out of the mountain, leading up to the massive castle.

"Alright, this is where your training begins" said Alex as he handed me the large hiking backpack filled with the supplies he bought at the market place. He put the bag on my back. It almost made me topple over it was so heavy.

"We start now?" I asked

"Yes, your first task is to make up the mountain carrying this bag. You have until sundown to make up the castle gates"

"Where you going? You're not coming with me?"

"I'll be waiting for you at the castle gates, don't keep me waiting too long"

Before I could get another word out, Alex was gone, leaving me standing there with this massive hiking bag on my back. The sun was directly over me so I assumed it was noon. I didn't know how far I had to go so I began my journey up the stone staircase.

OUTSIDE THE CASTLE GATES

Appearing in front of the castles iron gates, Alex cautiously pushed them open as he entered the castle grounds. The castle was well kept as if someone was still occupying the grounds. The castle was made of black Oak and trimmed in gold. The family crest of a golden dragon was mounted on the double doors of the entrance. He opened the double doors that lead into the throne room of the castle. Alex focused his senses as he searched the premises for any sign of life.

"I know you're here, I see you have gotten better at masking your scent" said Alex as he slowly walked towards the main hall searching the room with his eyes. The main room was a massive area with wooden pillars that ran the length of the room. The walls had scrolls with images of landscapes hanging from them. At the back of the room was a shrine. In the center of this shrine was a sword surrounded by candles and Sakura flowers.

"I see you found my sword" said Alex as he approached the shrine. Alex stood in front of the shrine where the sword sat peacefully. The sword's hilt was wrapped with leather ropes and its sheath was a matte black. Alex was hesitant to pick up the weapon. As he slowly reached out to touch the sword, he could feel the presence of another.

"Watashi wa kono tame ni 20-nen o matteimasu", said a voice coming from behind Alex.

"Has it been twenty years? And could you please speak English"

Standing before Alex was an oriental man dressed in the traditional black and orange garments of the monks in that area. He was about 5'5"; his black hair was in a long ponytail. In his hand, he held an iron staff. "I've been training for the past twenty years for our rematch Alex-son" replied the monk with his Japanese accent.

"Tamotsu, you still upset about that? I won fair and square", said Alex as smiled.

Tamotsu started twirling his staff, spinning it over his head, around his back and into his fighting stance.

"Grab your weapon Alex-son" replied Tamotsu as his eyes began to glow a luminous red.

"You know how I feel about using weapons" replied Alex as he crossed his arms as a gesture that he will not fight.

Tamotsu starts twirling his iron staff from side to side slowly.

"I'm not going to fight you Tamotsu; we already know how this is going to end. You're just not fast enough to keep up with me, it's a thirty-year gap between us and I'm a hybrid" said Alex. Tamotsu grinned at Alex as he began to twirl his staff faster. Alex could sense Tamotsu power growing.

"What are you up to Tamotsu?" said Alex as he uncrossed his arms. Tamotsu was now moving his staff with lightning speed. The iron staff made a whistling sound as it traveled around Tamotsu making an impenetrable shield.

"What the ...."

Before Alex could finish his sentence, Tamotsu leaped towards him bringing his staff over his head. Using an overhand grip, he tried to hit Alex like he was a nail and his staff was the hammer. Alex was caught off guard, but was able to sidestep at the last second. Tamotsu's staff hit the floor where Alex was standing with a thunderous sound leaving a crater in the wooden floor. Alex looked at Tamotsu wide eyed and confused. "How was Tamotsu able to increase his speed and strength so drastically?" Alex thought to himself.

Tamotsu yanked his staff out of the wooden floor sending pieces of wood flying through the air.

Alex leaped back to gain some distance but Tamotsu wasn't going to let him get away so easily. Tamotsu moved so quickly it appeared like he teleported beside Alex.

"Are you going to transform and fight me or should I just kill you now" replied Tamotsu as he swung his staff. He was moving too fast for Alex to attack; his only course of action was to block the attack by making an X with his forearms in front of him. The staff made a loud clung sound as the staff hit Alex forearm. The force of the attack sent Alex flight across the room smashing into the shrine and through the wall causing the wood to explode as Alex flew through it.

Tamotsu held his weapon at the ready, "I see you are still afraid to get angry, haven't you learned anything my student" said Tamotsu as he waited for Alex to appear from the debris. Searching with his eyes through the dust as pieces of broken wood falling from the shattered wall; Tamotsu found what he was looking for. Staring back at him through the dust cloud was a pair of glowing red eyes as the faint sound of a low audible growl echoed through the room.

Alex emerged from the dust and debris holding the sword that once rested peacefully on its shrine.

"Now control your anger Alex-son, just like this", said Tamotsu as he plunged his staff into the wooden floor. He took a deep breath as he began his transformation. Alex stood motionless as he watched Tamotsu change into his second form. Tamotsu now was a man with wolf features, long claws, slightly pointed ears, and a strong brow.

Tamotsu inhaled deep then unleashed a roar that echoed through the temple.

"Now show me your transformation Alex-son, don't be afraid. Or shall I force it out of you?"

Alex closed his eyes, his breathing heavy. When he opened them, his eyes still glowing a bright ruby red but the whites of his eyes were black which gave Alex a demonic appearance. This was the first time Alex had changed into his second form in thirty years. The last time he changed his rage made him slip into his final form; losing control resulted in the near destruction of the village and the annihilation of the vampire monk brethren that once occupied this temple.

Tamotsu and Alex stood motionless, staring at each other with a murderous look in their eyes. Alex was now in his second form with his animal like features in his face, more facial hair on his cheeks, pointed ears, razor sharp claws and fangs. Tamotsu snatches his staff out of the wooden floor, twirling it as he crouches into his fighting stance. "I see you are ready to take me seriously now" growled Tamotsu. Alex didn't speak as he stared at Tamotsu.

Tamotsu charged Alex, spinning his staff at his side. Alex didn't flinch. Tamotsu grab his staff with an overhand grip as he swung it at Alex. Without removing his sword from its sheath, Alex blocked Tamotsu's attack. The force from the attack shook the temple walls. Tamotsu continued his assault, spinning and twirling his staff striking high then immediately striking low trying to catch Alex off guard. It was like Tamotsu was attacking Alex from all angles, but Alex just blocked and evaded his opponent. The monk tried to stab Alex with the staff to create some distance between them but Alex pivoted on his back foot, turning him sideways as Tamotsu's iron staff barely grazes Alex as he spins. Tamotsu is left vulnerable to attack. Using the momentum, Alex spin kicks Tamotsu in his side sending him flying across the room.

Tamotsu hits the ground hard as his body ricochet across the ground like a pebble being skipped across a lake. Tamotsu rolled back to his feet as he dug his claws into the floor sliding to a halt. Alex stood awaiting his opponent holding his weapon at his side. Tamotsu lets out a loud roar and charged at Alex.

THE MOUNTAIN SIDE

Making her way up the mountain post heist, Raven jogged up the stone steps of the mountainside. She has been running for what felt like hours and she hasn't made it half way. She was beginning to get upset. She wanted to be trained, but she didn't think she would be dressed like a monk climbing a mountain with a hundred-pound backpack strapped to her back. The further she traveled up the mountain it began to get cooler. Down in the village the weather was a hot summers day, but now it was more like a cool spring day. Raven wiped the sweat from her brow using the sleeve of her robes. Without a watch or her phone, she had no idea what time it was or how long she had been climbing these steps.

Her shoulders began to ache from the weight of the backpack. She adjusted her straps as she admired the view of the village high on the mountain side. Taking in the scenery, she's never been outside of the city, but now she was standing on a mountain in the middle of the countryside of Japan about to learn the ancient ways of the werewolf. She didn't think in a million years any of this was possible. Things like this only existed in the pages of the novels she loved to read.

As Raven began to get lost in thought she was interrupted by a loud boom that came from the top of the mountain, followed by a roar. Raven's eyes lit up their bright yellow hue as she looked up to the mountain top. Without a second thought she started sprinting up the stone staircase. All she could think about was if Alex was in trouble. She was no longer concerned about the heavy backpack on her back or how much further she had to go. All she knew was that she had to get to the top. As she got closer to the top she could now pick up the scent of another, a werewolf. She felt the power emanating from up above, it was a terrifying feeling. She has never felt such a thing. She could feel Alex's emotions, he was angry, yet he was also scared but of what.

Raven continued her sprint up the mountain when she came to a part of stairs that had collapsed, leaving a huge gap that she was unable to clear. Raven didn't stop, her instincts took over. Raven leaped alongside the mountain, running across the wall. She extended her claws to scale the side of the mountain, abandoning the stone stair path. She cut her travel time in half by climbing up the mountainside. She finally made it to the top of the mountain a few feet from the temple gate. She rushed through the gates heading towards the sound of the battle. When she made it into the temple passed the large temple doors, entering the large room, she couldn't believe her eyes.

The room was a complete disaster. Dust and debris filled the air; one of the walls had collapsed, while another wall had a large hole in it. Some the wood pillars in the center of the room were shattered and splintered. It was a surprise the ceiling hadn't caved in yet. She searched the room with her eyes through the dust trying to find Alex. In the far corner of the room she found a pair of glowing red eyes looking back at her through the dust. Raven could feel it wasn't Alex. Emerging from the dusty shadows was a large silver wolf. It wasn't like a regular wolf; this silver wolf was the height of an average man.

Raven stood still, her heart racing as the silver wolf stalked her, waiting for her to move. The silver wolf began to slowly approach Raven as he growled. Raven had succumbed to fear, she never seen a werewolf before let alone an Alpha. The silver wolf stood up on its hind legs easily towering seven feet tall. He let out a roar that shook Raven out of her werewolf form. She covered her ears as her glowing yellow eyes returned to their normal brown. Appearing in front of her out of thin air stood Alex back in his human form and gripping a sword still in its sheath, "She is with me" he replied.

The silver wolf tilted its head as it looked at Alex with curiosity. "So that's why you vanished" growled the silver wolf. Raven watched as the silver wolf shrunk back to his human form. What remained standing in front of her was a shirtless Japanese man with his long black hair in a ponytail wearing black pants.

Alex turned to Raven, kneeling down to her, as she sat on the ground still in shock. "Are you ok?" asked Alex. Raven nodded yes as Alex helped her on her feet.

"Raven I would like to introduce to you my oldest friend and teacher Tamotsu Kishimoto."

Tamotsu bowed, "I do apologize about the scare. It has been a very long time since I've had visitors" replied Tamotsu

"Is she....?"

Alex nodded yes.

"But I thought......."

"I know, it's complicated" said Alex.

"Alright, so what brings you here?

"I thought you were lonely here in this dusty old temple so I thought you would like some company" smiled Alex.

"She needs training?" asked Tamotsu.

"Yes, she has anger issues, and what better way than to learn from a master?"

"I'm no master, besides I've taught you everything I know, you should be more than capable to teach her"

"True, but I need to be trained too. I think I found them and I need to be ready if I'm gonna take on a blue blood. Plus, I need to know how you improved so much. If you train us, I'll give you that real fight you always wanted"

Tamotsu thought about it for a moment as he caressed his chin. "Ok I'll train you two" replied Tamotsu.

Alex jumped for joy, excited about being trained. "Great! When do we......"

Before Alex could finish his sentence, Raven turned around, making her way out of the temple. "Raven!" shouted Alex, as she continued walking away. Raven made it out of the temple speed walking towards the iron entry gates, when Alex teleports in front of the gates blocking her exit.

"Where are you going?"

"What the hell was that??!?! That little Asian man was about to kill me! Am I gonna turn into monster like that!? And why was I able to feel your emotional state?? I thought you were in trouble?!? I don't even remember how I got up the mountain so fast"

"Calm down, you are safe. Like I said that little Asian man is my friend Tamotsu. We were sparring. He was testing me and no, you won't turn into a monster. You're a beta, so you are unable to fully transform, that's an Alpha's ability…"

"Can you turn like that?"

"Yes, but I haven't in a very long time…."

"Is that what you were afraid of?

"Just between me and you, yes. The reason you are able to sense me and feel my emotions is because of our pack link. It gives us an advantage when we are hunting or fighting. Now you said you wanted to learn how to fight and control your powers, what better way than with a monk warrior from the nineteenth century? Plus, I'll be right beside you every step of the way" smiled Alex

Raven didn't respond as she thought over the things Alex just told her. She did want to learn to defend herself and control these new powers. "Alright, but you have to train with me" she said.

"I'll never leave your side, scout's honor" smiled Alex as he raised his right hand.

"Shut up, you too big to be a boy scout" replied Raven as she cracked a slight smile.

Raven and Alex returned inside the temple were Tamotsu was sitting in on the ground legs crossed, eyes closed taking slow deep breaths.

"Is everything alright?" said Tamotsu calmly.

"Yeah, she's cool now, we had a little talk and everything is fine" said Alex.

Tamotsu jumped up from his sitting position landing gently on his feet. "Good, follow me"

Tamotsu lead Raven and Alex down a long hallway lit by candle light. As they made their way through the hallway they passed empty rooms that looked like they haven't been occupied in a very long time.

Mr. Tamostu, where are the other monks? Do you really live here alone?

Tamotsu never looked back at Raven as he continued walking. "They're all dead" replied Tamotsu.

EPISODE 7

"TRAINING DAY"

The trio came to the end of the hallway that led into another large open space. Like the rest of the temple there were no windows. The room was filled with wooden dummies, punching bags, speed bags and other various training equipment. One wall was covered with hanging scrolls that had images of men demonstrating different fighting stances and techniques, while the opposite wall looked like an armory, with an assortment of weapons from Katanas, nun chucks, wooden staffs and other unique weapons.

"Before we get started I'll tell you how I was able to improve my strength and speed" said Tamotsu.

"Wait, don't change the subject, what happened to the other monks?" asked Raven.

Alex tapped her on the shoulder shaking his head no. Raven looked back at him, "What, what happen?"

"I'll make you a deal, once you have been trained then I will share with you the fate of my brethren" said Tamotsu.

"So, all I have to do is train with you two and that's it?"

"That's it…" replied Tamotsu

Raven looks back at Alex as he shrugs his shoulders.

"Now where was I" said Tamotsu. "Oh yes, now I remember". Tamotsu walked over to the wall with large variety of weapons. He grabs a dark oak wood box with the same dragon symbol that was on the gates of the temple.

"As a royal guard my duty, like Alex-son, was to protect, and when I was unable to do to so, due to my lack of power. I went in search to become stronger. As werewolves, we lack the ability get stronger as fast as vampires. We still have to physically exercise to get stronger; they simply just have to age to become stronger. Even as an Alpha I'm still limited to the rate in which I get stronger. Then I had these made" Tamotsu opened the wooden box, inside were four iron bracelets with Japanese characters engraved in them.

"Bracelets? You got stronger by wearing jewelry?" asked Raven.

"Not just any bracelets my Chisana okami, these are magical weighted bracelets" replied Tamotsu.

"What did you call me? What did he say?" asked a confused Raven.

Alex chuckled. "He called you little wolf"

"Oh, that's kind of cute, I like it"

Tamotsu placed the iron bracelets on Ravens wrist and on her ankles. Raven slightly shivered as the cold metal touched her skin. Raven admired the bracelets, "I thought these were supposed to be weighted Mr. Tamotsu?"

"I haven't said the magical incantation" replied Tamotsu as he walked back over to the wall of weapons. "I knew once you heard of this new technique you would want your own pair Alex-son, so I had these made specifically for you. He brought Alex a larger wooden box. Inside was a pair of iron shackles with similar Japanese characters on it. Filled with excitement, Alex grabbed them a placed them on his ankles and wrist.

"Look Raven we have matching sets" smiled Alex.

"Now that you are ready let's begin, Shiru!" shouted Tamotsu. Suddenly Raven and Alex's iron bracelets locked tightly and sealed, making them look seamless as if they were apart of them.

"Wait, how do I get these off?" asked Raven nervously.

Tamotsu ignored her question as he continued his lesson. "Chisana Okami, once I'm done training you, you could be as strong as me"

"Really?? asked Raven excitedly.

"Yes, if my suspicions are correct. As for you Alex-son, there is nothing more I can teach you. However, I have a special task for you while I train Chisana Okami"

"You don't have some secret techniques or some ancient scroll" said Alex.

Tamotsu shook his head no, "But I'm interested in seeing how much you improve, you aren't like us, you're a hybrid. Your potential could be limitless."

"I still can't believe wearing weights could improve your speed and strength in such a short time" said Alex.

"Yeah, he has a point…." said Raven.

Tamotsu walked up to Alex and placed his had gently on Alex's bracelets. He looked Alex in the eyes as he gave him an evil grin. Alex started to feel his bracelets pulling him towards the ground. He started to struggle standing up right as gravity tugged at him. "That's all you got Tamotsu, I thought this was going to be a challenge" grunted Alex. Impressed at Alex's strength, Tamotsu leaned in close to Alex so Raven was unable to hear his next words, "Impressive Alex-son, but let's see how you do with your body weight at 2-tons"

"Wait what?" before Alex could respond the weight from his bracelets sent him forcefully to the ground with a loud boom. Down on his hands and knees Alex struggled to stay upright.

"You're killing him!" shouted Raven as she rushes over to aid Alex. Tamotsu steps in front Raven blocking her from getting to Alex.

"He is immortal he will not die" said Tamotsu.

"It's ok Raven, I'll be fine" grunted Alex trying sound calm. His body felt like it was being crushed. His bones felt like they could snap at any moment, as every muscle in his body burned while struggling to hold his body up. Tamotsu kneeled down in front of Alex, "I'm surprised you're still conscious" whispered Tamotsu. "You will survive this, and when you do you will be stronger than you have ever been. Even now as your body is being destroyed under all this pressure, I can hear your body healing rapidly. Just like working any muscle it has to be broken down and repair itself to become stronger to handle the stress. Oh, one more thing try to transform, I want to see if you can handle this in your transformed state."

Alex struggles to lift his head up to look at Tamotsu, "Not in front of her, I don't want her to get hurt if I lose control"

Tamotsu looks back at Raven who watches Alex struggle with worried eyes. "As you wish Alex-son" replied Tamotsu. Rising to his feet, leaving Alex where he was barely keeping himself from collapsing to the ground.

"Coming with me little wolf we have work to do"

"What about Alex?"

"He will be fine"

Tamotsu lead Raven out of the training room, before exiting the room Raven looked back at Alex. She could feel him struggling as he fought the urge to transform in front of her. She still couldn't understand why she was able to feel what he was feeling. She wondered if he felt what she was feeling as well. She followed Tamotsu down another hallway that took them outside the temple walls. Standing beside Tamotsu outside, Raven was blown away by the scenery. She found herself looking at a beautiful rock garden located in the back of the temple. The rock garden was surrounded by lavish cherry blossom trees, a man-made waterfall that ran into a small pond filled gorgeous pink and white koi fish. The garden was a massive rectangle shape, the length of a football field. Placed within it were thirteen stones of different sizes, carefully composed in five groups; one group of five, one group of three and two groups of two. The stones were surrounded by white gravel that hasn't been racked.

"Mr. Tamotsu this is beautiful" gasped Raven taking in the majestic sight of the rock garden. "But isn't the garden supposed to have those lines going thru it"

"Very observant little wolf, those lines are to represent ripples or waves in a body of water and the gravel represents that body of water. The reason we are here is so you can create those waves."

"Me?"

"Yes, this will help you focus. You will come here every day as part of your training"

"Mr. Tamotsu this thing is huge! It will take forever to rack this!"

"Then we should get started, but first we need to get you accustomed to wearing the weights.

Tamotsu walked towards Raven to activate her bracelets when a loud roar came from the temple followed by a booming sound that shook the very ground. It felt like something gigantic was moving through the temple halls making its way towards Raven and Tamotsu. The two werewolves looked back at the door that led into the temple as the booming sound became louder and louder as it approached.

"Impossible" said Tamotsu dumbfounded.

"Is that…?" asked Raven as Tamotsu shock his head yes.

Emerging from the hall drenched in sweat, stood Alex in his second werewolf form. Breathing heavily, he searched the temple garden with his eyes until he found his prey, as Tamotsu and Alex made eye contact. Alex took a breath, inhaling deeply then released a roar so loud, that Raven and even Tamotsu covered his ears.

"Alex-son, don't let your anger get the best of you, calm down" replied Tamotsu in a calm voice as he slowly approached him.

Alex felt a sharp pain in his abdomen that made him buckle. He fell to his knees with such force it felt like a small tremor.

"Mr. Tamotsu what's wrong with Alex?"

"Stay back little wolf, Alex is becoming consumed with anger. I think he is about to change into his final form"

"Wait, he has another form?"

"Yes, you remember when you saw me in my wolf form? Well as an Alpha we can morph into a wolf. But unlike me, Alex isn't able to control his beast form due to his vampire side. If he changes he will go into a blood lusting rage" said Tamotsu as he slowly approached Alex.

Down on his knees, clutching his stomach, Alex had begun his transformation into his final form. His skin started to change from its chocolate complexion, to a dark grey hue. Black fur began to cover his back, shoulders and arms, only leaving his chest and abdominals uncovered. The fur wasn't thick like a wolf but more like the coat of a black lion, sleek and shiny. When Alex looked up, the whites of his eyes were replaced by pure darkness leaving only the burning ruby red pupils to be visible.

At this moment Tamotsu knew it was too late, Alex was lost, consumed by rage. Raven watched in terror as Alex stood up slowly making eye contact with only Tamotsu.

"Alex-son, I know you're in there, I need you fight it!"

Alex started to phase in and out but wasn't able to disappear. He looked down at his hands, confused why he didn't teleport.

"I forgot to mention, the bracelets disable your ability to teleport" replied Tamotsu. "Now don't make me do this, there is no honor in fighting you like this"

Alex didn't respond. He looked down at the iron bands that were around his ankles and wrist, deciding what his next course of action would be. Then he looked back at Tamotsu with the intent to kill in his eyes as he lifted his two-ton legs to walk. Alex no longer moved with incredible speed, he walked like a giant with slow earth trembling footsteps.

"You leave me no choice Alex-san" said Tamotsu softly as he morphed his hand into his clawed werewolf hand. Sprinting towards his friend, claws drawn, Tamotsu couldn't help but be reminded of the last time Alex turned into a raging beast. As Tamotsu got closer, Alex extending his arm back to punch; his movements slowed due to the massive weight of his bracelets. With no hesitation Tamotsu reached out with his clawed hand, jabbing his claws into Alex chest to attack his pressure points that would knock Alex unconscious, but at the last-minute Alex tried to teleport. Like before he didn't teleport, instead he phased in and out allowing Tamotsu's clawed hand to go straight through him as if Alex was a ghost. Caught off guard by this new and unexpected ability, Tamotsu was left vulnerable for an attack. Before he could react, Alex rematerialized punching Tamotsu with the force of two tons, sending Tamotsu hurling through the air like a crash test dummy into the serene rock garden. White sand and broken shards of the huge stones scattered as Tamotsu's body destroyed the peaceful arrangement as he bounced and slid through the length of the rock garden.

Raven watched in horror as Alex marched towards Tamotsu's unconscious body lying in the rubble of the rock garden. Afraid that Alex would kill Tamotsu, Raven rushed over to stand between Alex and a badly beaten Tamotsu.

"Alex, snap out of it, this isn't you" shouted Raven as tears formed in her eyes. Her cries fell on deaf ears as the monster, which was Alex unhurriedly marched towards Raven.

"If Tamotsu couldn't stop him, how am I" thought Raven to herself as she tried to figure out a way to get through to Alex. With no more time to think, Alex stood in front of her looking down at her with his glowing demonic red eyes.

"Don't do this Alex; I know you're in there. You don't want to hurt me, do you?"

Alex began to growl then let out a roar. Raven didn't flinch as the force from the roar felt like she was standing in the downdraft of a helicopter propeller. Raven wasn't going to lose Alex to his anger, but she didn't know how to reach him. Then suddenly a thought came to her. She vaguely remembered what Alex did to get her out of her rage induced trance. "But would it work" she thought to herself. With no other options, she went with her gut feeling. She looked up into Alex's cold, dark ruby red eyes as her own eyes began to glow bright yellow. She inhaled deeply, then released a roar that made Alex flinch slightly as the whites began to return to his eyes, but he quickly shook it off. In the time, it took Alex to return his focus, a badly beaten Tamotsu jumped up from behind Raven hitting Alex in specific pressure points on his chest, instantly causing Alex to collapse, sending his two-ton body crashing to the ground.

"Mr.Tamotsu! You're alive!" said Raven as she helps Tamotsu to his feet. "What did you do to him?"

"It's called *the dragon's touch*" replied Tamotsu. "It's the same move I used the last time Alex had an episode. I basically hit several vital points shutting off his heart...."

"You killed him?!?" shouted Raven, as she lets Tamotsu stumble back the ground.

"Don't worry little wolf, he will wake up soon. Alex-son isn't like you and me, he is immortal"

"How long will he be out?" said Raven, deeply concerned about Alex.

"It depends on how fast his body heals from the trauma of *the dragon's touch*. For now let's go into the temple, I need to heal myself before he wakes, he might be a little grumpy after losing."

"We're just gonna leave him out here?"

"He will be fine, plus he currently weighs 2-ton. Besides, there is a full moon in five days and I need to prepare you for."

Raven assisted Tamotsu into the temple, leaving a lifeless Alex laying in the wake of the destruction he caused. As they made their way into the temple, down the long corridor filled by candle light, Raven had a thought.

"Mr. Tamotsu, if Alex is dead, does that mean he is in heaven, or…."

"That's a good question little wolf. Some say there's a different place we supernatural go once we die. Honestly, I don't know. We will have to ask him when he returns"

"Alexander, Aaaallleeexxaaannndeer, wake up sleepy head" The sound of a familiar, angelic voice combined with the sweet nostalgic aroma of lavender and honey pulled him from his unconscious state. With his eyes still closed, he could feel a gentle touch making circles on his chest with their finger. Their cold hands made Alex release a low growl. He slowly opened his eyes, taking a peek at his surroundings, to find himself lying on his back looking up at the ceiling of the wooden carriage. To his left, lying next to him, dressed in a white nightgown, her hand caressing his chest was Princess Isis.

"I must be dreaming…" said Alex as he stretched

Isis rested her head on his chest, "No my love, you are not dreaming, it's really me"

Alex lets out a soft chuckle, "This is a dream."

"Ok, then tell me what's the last thing you remember?"

Alex closed his eyes as he rested on the pile of soft Egyptian cotton blankets that were placed in the center of the carriage floor. Suddenly his mind was flooded with images of him attack Tamotsu and nearly hurting Raven. He sat up quickly as his memory returned, "Holy shit! So that means…"

Isis nods her head yes.

"So, you are really?"

Before she could respond Alex pulled her close, resting his head on her chest. He hugged her tightly as he fought back his tears. "I've missed you so much"

"I've missed you too my love, but we don't have much time"

"What do you mean?"

"I felt your presents here in between the living world and the Afterlife, so I came here to see you"

"So, this is like the waiting room to enter the Afterlife? So why haven't I completely passed over?"

"Even though you're dead, your body is already healing, so you will be awakening soon. I've been watching you over the past years my love and you have been a bad boy. This isn't the Alexander I fell in love with. You are still harboring the feelings of losing me and it's affecting your subconscious. It's the reason you are unable to control your new form."

"So, what am I supposed to do? Just forget what they have done to us? No, they deserve to die, they will pay"

"I'm not saying let them live, I want you to kill every last one of them, but first you must let go and deal with the pain of losing me. Even if I didn't die that night we could never be."

Even though Alex knew this to be true, hearing her say the words aloud hurt. He felt as if his heart was being split into two. Isis could see the hurt on his face. She caressed his face, gently running her fingers across his lips.

"Now Alexander, you know that I love you more than words can express, but I had a duty to my people, I had to preserve my bloodline, and now you are all that's left. So, I need you to let me go so that you can reach your full potential. You are all that's left of both my bloodline and yours.

"I understand your majesty" replied Alex refusing to make eye contact.

Isis lifted Alex head up by placing her finger under his chin. "Alexander……"

Alex looked into her eyes with a sad puppy dog look on his face.

"Don't look at me like that; you know this is what has to be done. Now promise, you will deal with your issues, not just for you but for your beta's sake."

"You know about her?" said Alex surprisingly.

"I told you, I've been watching you. She's cute I think she is a suitable mate"

"Isis!!"

"What? I want you to be happy, she is good for you, she kind of reminds me of myself. I approve of her."

Alex started to fade in and out of existence. "What's happening to me?"

"It looks like we are out of time; your body is reviving you."

"No, I need more time…"

"There is no more time. I don't want to see you back over here Alexander. Take care of your beta and be a great Alpha like your mother."

Isis grabbed Alexander by the face, kissing him softly as he fades away, leaving her sitting alone in their carriage. As a tear begins to fall down her cheek she smiles. "Give them hell my love"

Back at the temple

"Where are we?" asked Raven as she escorted Tamotsu into another room deep within the temple.

"This is where one comes for deep meditation. Once in this room all outside sound is blocked out by a magical spell giving you complete concentration and focus. In this room, you will learn how to sense the presence of supernatural beings. As soon as they crossed the threshold into the circular room, everything became completely silent. The room was bathed in the soft light of a thousand candles as the gentle sound of the flickering flames of the candles filled the room.

"Wow, you weren't playing, I can't hear any outside noise" said Raven

"I'll take it from here 'Little Wolf" replied Tamotsu.

Tamotsu took his arm from around Raven's shoulder, applying most of his weight on his good leg as he limped to the center of the room. He slowly sat himself on one of two hand woven rugs that sat in the center of the meditation room.

"Come sit Little Wolf", replied Tamotsu making himself comfortable. Raven sat on the rug facing Tamotsu, crossing her legs.

"Little Wolf, when you are out there in the real world, you are going to come across a variety of supernatural beings. Now once you complete your training you will be capable of taking care of yourself if anyone tries to test you, but even after all this training there will be those you just won't be able to defeat. As a werewolf your senses are heightened, which I'm sure you have noticed by now. Just like any animal in the wild you have a natural ability to sense danger or the presence of other beings."

"You mean like a six sense?" asked Raven.

"For a lack of a better word, yes it's like a six sense. I'll give you an example, close your eyes and focus on your surroundings."

Raven did as she was told, closing her eyes, as she began to focus on the calming sound of the flicker flames of the burning candles.

"Focus on the flickering of the flames, take slow, deep breathes clear your mind of all thoughts" said Tamotsu in a calm hypnotizing voice. Raven tried to clear her mind but worrying about Alex was making it hard for her to focus. After a few moments of trying to focus, Raven started to get restless.

"Mr. Tamotsu, this isn't working I'm not sensing or feeling……"

Suddenly she felt something; it was subtle like a tiny blip on radar.

"What were you saying...?"

"Shhh... I felt something. Is that you Mr. Tamotsu??

"Very good, what else do you notice? smiled Tamotsu

Raven focused harder, biting the bottom of her lip as she concentrated, trying to expand her awareness.

"It feels like a warm vibration."

"Excellent, I was hiding my presents from you that's why it was difficult to sense me. Now let me show you what it feels like when I'm not hiding my presents."

Tamotsu took a deep breath, then let out a huge sigh as if he just released the weight of the world off his shoulders.

Raven gasped as she felt Tamotsu's presents. It was the same feeling she had when she first felt his presents during his fight with Alex in the ceremony room. She didn't understand what she felt then but now she knew that fear she felt was her senses telling her she was in the presents of danger.

"I remember this feeling, from the first time we met when you were in fighting Alex. Your presents feel heavy, dense, and much different from the warm, vibrations from before"

"Very good, now that's just a sample of what you will experience in the real world. Everyone feels different, but what will always stay consistent is the presence of a great power. It will always feel heavy, dense, intimidating. Tamotsu continued his lecture about the sensing and feeling your opponent's power, when suddenly Raven felt the presence of another.

"Mr. Tamotsu, something is coming" shouted Raven anxiously. Hoping it was Alex finally resurrected, as it got closer to their location she realized it was an unfamiliar presents.

"Oh, I'm surprised you noticed. I'm impressed"

"It's not Alex, whoever it is their heading this way and moving fast"

Raven, with her eyes closed focused on the approaching power heading towards them.

"It's not human; it's a werewolf, not as strong as you, so I assume it's a beta. I didn't know there were other werewolves here?" replied a confused Raven.

The presents of the mysterious werewolf was a few feet away from the entrance of the meditation room, Raven opened her eyes to see who this person was. Standing in the doorway stood a young Japanese man who looked around the same age as Raven; dressed in similar ancient Samurai armor as the old man she met who was standing guard at the entrance of the bamboo forest.

"Sensei, I heard the call of a wolf! I came as fast as I could. What happened to the ceremony room?" the young warrior asked. He quickly removed his straw hat to reveal his slender, youthful face. "Who is that?? What is going on here Sensei??"

"So nice of you to join us," replied Tamotsu as he stood up. Raven followed his lead. "Akio, I would like to introduce you to my new student and Alex-sons, beta Raven"

"Yes!" shouted Akio. "Finally, someone I can spare with and…. Wait; did you just say Alex-sons beta?? Is he here??"

"Mr. Tamotsu, who is he?? Raven asked.

"Oh, how rude of me, my name is Akio, apprentice of Sensei Tamotsu and his beta." said Akio proudly as he bowed to Raven. Raven returned the gesture by bowing.

"Mr. Tamotsu said that all the monks died."

"They are. I witnessed the annihilation of the vampire monks all those years ago" replied Akio

"After I stopped Alex-son, Akio begged me to make him like me and teach him martial arts. I was hesitant at first, but his persistence won me over so I gave him the bite"

"I've been training ever since waiting for the day I can use what I've learned in battle! With you here, hopefully you will be a worthy opponent."

Akio continued his rant about how excited he was that Tamotsu had taken on a new student, and all the fun Raven and he will have training when Raven started to sense something coming. It was faint but it was there. She looked around to see if Akio and Tamotsu noticed it, but they didn't seem to notice.

"Do you guys feel that?" asked Raven, interrupting the conversation that Akio was clearly having with himself.

"Feel what?" asked Tamotsu.

Without answering him, Raven plopped back down on the floor, immediately crossing her legs and shutting her eyes. Akio and Tamotsu exchanged confused looks to one another.

"Is she ok Sensei?"

Raven sat focused, deep in concentration as Akio and Tamotsu watched in anticipation when suddenly Raven shouts, "He's back!"

Before anyone could get a word out, Raven was already on her feet, making a mad dash for the door, sprinting down the temple hallway, leaving Tamotsu and Akio in silence.

"She is a fast learner" smirked Tamotsu.

Maneuvering through the labyrinth, they call the temple hallways, Raven moved with uncanny speed. She moved so quickly, that when passing by a room filled with candles the force she created blew out the candles instantly. She made it back to the white sand garden that Alex destroyed hours earlier. She stood in the doorway hoping to see Alex on his feet, instead she found him lying lifeless where Mr. Tamotsu left him. She swore she could feel his presents, "maybe I still need more training" she thought to herself. Just when she was about to lose confidence in here abilities, Alex gasps for air then lets out a roar. Filled with joy and relief, Raven rushed to Alex side. He lied on the ground huffing and puffing as he tried to catch his breath. He struggled to get to his feet, due to still being under the pressure of the two-ton weights he still wore.

"Are you alright?? I didn't know Mr. Tamotsu was going to kill you!!" said Raven as she too struggled to help Alex to sit up.

"Ugh, yeah I'm fine, I didn't know I was going to die either" said Alex.

"Alex-son!!! You should've told me you were coming to train, I would have stayed here" shouted Akio excitedly as he and Tamotsu emerged from the temple.

"I see you met Akio" said Alex to Raven.

"Are you alright Alex-son?" as a concerned Tamotsu.

"I'm alright; I know you had to do what you had to. I'm just glad I didn't hurt anyone, or worse.

Tamotsu and the others helped Alex to his feet.

"I think we've had enough excitement for one day, let's get Alex-son into the temple to get some rest"

"No, I'm fine let's continue training"

"Are you crazy? You died and came back to life! You can barely stand on your own!" said a frustrated Raven

"She has a point" replied Akio.

"Get some rest. We can start tomorrow morning, bright and early, for now you must rest"

Alex knew he was in no shape to do anything, let alone train. "Fine, I'll rest, but tomorrow we train."

The next morning

Pacing back and forth in the center of the training mat, Tamotsu addressed Raven and the others as they sat legs crossed on the floor in front of him.

"Today, we begin your training. But before we get started, Alex-son there isn't anything more I can teach you as far as martial arts goes. For now, I had Akio and Han bring supplies from the village so you can start the repairs on the ceremony room and the sand garden.

"Wait, you telling me, you can't help me? Asked Alex

"What I'm saying is repairing the ceremony room and the rock garden is your first task."

"But...."

"No buts Alex-son, now go get started."

"Yes sensei," replied Alex. He hopped to his feet, bowed to Tamotsu then slowly marched out of the training room.

"Will he be alright Mr. Tamotsu?" asked Raven

"He will be fine; the task I gave him will help him get accustomed to the two-ton weights. As you can see he is already moving around more freely. Now let's get started with your training. Come forward little wolf."

Raven got to her feet and walked towards Tamotsu.

"Extend your arms"

Raven put her arms out in front of her showing bracelets.

"First thing first, I'll activate these bracelets" Tamotsu waved his hand across Ravens bracelets. They began to glow and with a flash of light they went from cute bracelets to iron gauntlets that ran from her wrist to her forearm. She began to feel the gravity around her pushing down on her. She struggled to stay upright under the pressure.

"You are now under two times your bodyweight" said Tamotsu. Raven felt like she weighed a ton. Her muscles burned as she tried to do the simplest of movements.

"Now let's begin. You need to become accustomed to the extra weight. Once you are able to move freely will move to the next lesson. Akio come forward. Little wolf, to help you get familiar with this weight, I want you to capture this bell from Akio's waist" said Tamotsu as he tied a pair of jingle bells on Akio's belt loop.

Raven watched as she was finally able to stand up right. "So, you want me to chase him around? I can barely get my arms over my head!"

"Little wolf, I have a theory I want to test out. And if I'm correct, buy the end of today you will capture these bells."

"Are your serious sensei?" asked Akio as he crossed his arms.

"Akio, this has nothing to do with your skill level. You are an exceptional warrior, but Raven is special. She is the beta of a hybrid there is no telling what she is capable of."

"Well this should be fun to see what she is really made of."

"Easy for you to say, you're not the one wearing the bracelets" said Raven sarcastically.

Akio smiled as he lifted up his sleeves. "Oh, you mean these?" Akio also wore a pair of magical bracelets. "You're not the first person to training with these bracelets. Well little wolf let's get started" smiled Akio.

"Remember little wolf, the faster you catch Akio, the faster we move on to the next lesson" said Tamotsu in a calm and assuring voice.

"At this rate, we will be here for months" said Akio as he let out a hearty chuckle.

Raven began to get frustrated as she struggled, marching slowly after Akio who was taunting her. Trying to figure out how she was going to catch Akio to end this tiring game, a thought came to her. She remembered what Alex did when he was dealing with these magical weights. She stopped chasing Akio and stood motionless as she took a deep breath.

"Little wolf giving up already?" taunted Akio using a baby voice.

"I need more power" said Raven repeatedly in her head. When she opened her eyes, they glowed their luminous yellow.

"Oooh, looks like someone is starting to take this seriously.

Raven growls as she rushes towards Akio. Her speed shocked Akio but she was still not fast enough. She slashed and clawed at Akio desperately trying to capture the bells.

"You gotta be quicker than that little wolf if you want to catch me" replied Akio as he performed a series of back flips creating distance between Raven and himself.

Filled with rage, Raven let another roar as she transformed into her final form.

Tamotsu watched, intrigued by Ravens progress. "She is getting stronger faster than I expected" Tamotsu thought to himself.

"That's more like it" said Akio as he was filled with excitement.

Raven was now in here werewolf form, with her longs razor sharp claws, and wolf like features in her face. She was now able to move freely with her weights but still no match for Akio.

She lunged at him, the sudden burst of speed caught Akio off guard. At the last moment Akio pivoted to his right allowing Raven to pass by him crashing into the wooden training dummies. The wooden dummies shattered like glass from the force of Ravens heavy body colliding into them.

"I need more power" said Raven over and over to herself in her head.

"How are you doing this?" asked Akio "You're better than I thought but you still not good enough"

Raven shook the wooden debris off of her, letting out a low audible growl. "Akio when I get my hands on you" said Raven with the look of determination in her eyes. She launched herself off the ground towards Akio clawing and slashing at him as they continued their game of cat and mouse.

Rubbing his temples as he entered the training room, Alex replied "Tamotsu what the…."

Tamotsu puts his finger on his lip, letting Alex know to be quiet. Then he pats the seat next to him. Alex walked over to Tamotsu then sat down.

"Tamotsu, I can hear Raven calling to me, asking for power" whispered Alex as he watched his beta train.

Tamotsu rubbed his chin, "What you are experiencing is called Pack Link Alex-Son. You and little wolf must have a strong connection. If you can focus, you will be able to give her power through battle meditation"

"Really?"

"I forgot you never been a part of a pack. I guess I do have more to teach you. Close your eyes and clear your mind. Now, focus on Raven. Feel the connection between you" replied Tamotsu.

Alex was able to feel what Raven was feeling. He felt her pain, her frustration.

"She is in pain, frustrated. She needs my help" whispered Alex.

"Good, now if you want, you can ease her pain, by taking it on yourself. Just remember if you take on too much you may cause your own issues."

"I'm aware Tamotsu; I will not lose control again. I need to be stronger for her" said Alex.

He took a deep breath, and then Alex opened himself up allowing Ravens pain into himself as he gave her some his power. Alex grunted as he felt Raven's pain flooded his mind.

"Be careful Alex-son"

"I got this. I can't be the Alpha she needs if I can't control myself. So, shut up and let me concentrate" barked Alex.

Tamotsu smiled

Chasing Akio around the room, Raven began to feel fatigue setting in. Her movements were now slow and sloppy, her breathing was heavy. She stopped, slumped over, placing her hands on her knees trying to catch her breath.

"What's the matter? You tired already? You are too young to be tired already. I haven't even got to use my transformation yet."

"Shut up Akio!" yelled Raven as she lunged at him. Akio just side stepped allowing Raven to fly past him. She crashed hard to the ground.

"I guess that's it for the beta of the legendary hybrid."

"When I get stronger I'm gonna wipe that stupid smirk off your face"

"HAHAHAHAHAHA, so feisty" replied Akio.

As Akio continued his rant, Raven began to feel the pain leaving her muscles. She felt rejuvenated, stronger than before. Confused, she looked towards where Tamotsu sat, that's when she saw Alex sitting next to him with legs crossed, in deep meditation.

"Is Alex doing this?" she asked herself.

"Are you giving up little wolf?" asked Akio

"I'm just getting started" replied Raven as she stood up.

"Good, I was ……"

Before he could finish his sentence, Raven charged him, catching him off guard. She was now moving much faster than before. She tackled Akio, sending them both crashing to the ground. Akio used the momentum, placing his foot on Raven's stomach, tossing her over him. Raven's instincts kicked in as she flipped and twisted in the air so that she would land on her feet.

Akio jumped back to his feet, "I don't know how you are doing this, but I like it" smiled Akio as he transformed into his final beta form.

"Now let's get serious" he snarled.

Raven charged Akio slashing and clawing at his waist, reaching for silver bells dangling from his belt loop. Akio bobbed and weaved, evading Ravens attempts.

Alex sat with his eyes closed. This new experience of the Pack Link was a new feeling. He was able to feel her pain, her frustration. The ability to share his power with her was also an amazing feeling as well as tiring. He had given her power but it was still not enough, and her voice echoed in the darkest corners of his mind repeating the same four words…" I NEED MORE POWER"

"Tamotsu, what would happen if I gave Raven more of my power?" asked Alex eyes still closed.

Normally, if you gave her too much power she could become stronger, but there is also the possibility that her body can't handle it and her muscles tear themselves apart" replied Tamotsu with a tone of caution in his voice.

"So, if I transform while in this pack link, will that give her more power?"

Tamotsu thought about it, He has never heard of an Alpha transforming while in battle meditation. "Theoretically it's possible, but can you handle the change? You remember what happened last time you transformed"

"I remember, but like I said, she needs me and I will NEVER lose control again. Besides she wouldn't be able to handle my power yet, so I'll just go to my second transformation. Alex starts to take slow and controlled breaths as he slipped into his second form. Tamotsu kept his eye on Alex. If he starts to lose control again, he will not hesitate to put Alex down again. Once Tamotsu was sure Alex wouldn't lose control, he turned his attention to Raven and Akio battling on the training mat. He started to notice Raven becoming faster as Akio was starting to lose his advantage over her.

"Amazing, said Tamotsu. Alex was in his second form and showed no signs of losing control; on top of that Raven is now moving effortlessly with her weights. The power Alex was giving off was remarkable. It felt like Tamotsu could be crushed under the pressure.

Akio was now becoming frustrated. Somehow Raven has become stronger. He was having a hard time keeping her away from her objective. At first, he was just evading her, but now he was calling on his martial art skills to block and deflect her attacks.

Akio now was fighting off Ravens attacks, and he was becoming even more frustrated. Unfocused on the task at hand Akio was becoming sloppy. Raven noticed it and took advantage of it. She slashed high at his face as a diversion. Akio leaned back to avoid getting his face ripped off. Then raven swiped at his waist. Unable to avoid her attack, Akio was left with only one choice. He kicked Raven in the chest sending her tumbling across the floor of the training mat.

Tamotsu jumped up from his sitting position, "Akio! Stand down; she is not trained for combat!"

"No! Let them fight" said Alex as he was still locked into his battle meditation. "This will be training for both of us"

"Are you sure Alex-son?"

Alex shock his head yes.

"Ok, but if this fight gets out of hand I will jump in and stop this immediately"

"Thank you, Alex-son," replied Akio as he stood in his fighting stance. "Get up little wolf, I know you still have a little fight left in you.

Raven jumps to her feet, closing her eyes. With her eyes still closed, she suddenly gets into a fighting stance. Tamotsu watches this puzzled. He knew this stance, and then he looked at Alex." Could he be giving Raven more than just his power, or has he taken control over Ravens body?"

Raven opened her eyes to find herself standing in the middle of nowhere, surrounded by white clouds. Off in the distance she saw Alex sitting on a black cloud still meditating. Raven walked over to him. Once she was close enough he began to speak.

"Before you ask, we are inside your mind. Please sit"

Clouds started gathering next to Raven forming a seat. She sat down on the cloud, to her disbelief the cloud was firmer than she expected.

"What's going on Alex?"

"Our minds are currently linked through a pack link. Tamotsu also showed me this battle meditation technique that's been giving you the boost of power."

"That does explain a lot. So why are we here?"

"Honestly I have no idea. You must have picked up on my presents or something. But forget all of that. Akio is about to kick yo ass and I'm not about to have that, so I want to see if I can guide you in the martials arts. We will fight as one."

"So, you want to control my body?"

"No, I want you to use my knowledge to fight him"

"You think it will work?

"It's only one way to find out. Close your eyes and concentrate. I think it's working."

"This is incredible; I think I know martial arts!" said Raven excitedly

"Good, now go show Akio how we Knights fight!"

When Raven opened her eyes, she was back standing in front of Akio on the training mat.

"What the hell is wrong with your eye? Is one of your eyes red?" asked Akio

Raven didn't say a word. She just charged Akio.

Tamotsu watched in awe. Never in all his years has he seen a connection as strong as Alex and Ravens. In the middle off the training mat Raven and Akio exchanged a series of punches and kicks. Akio blocked most of Ravens punches but left himself open to Ravens kicks. She connected with two swift kicks to Akio's stomach sending him crashing to the ground, tumbling several feet back. Akio hoppped back to his feet furious, unleashing a loud roar. Akio pulls his sword from its sheath then charges towards Raven. Tamotsu immediately jumps to his feet, but Alex grabs him by the arm. Tamotsu looks at Alex as if he had lost his mind. Alex simply shakes his head no. Tamotsu turned back to see how this would play out.

Raven stood her ground as Akio charged towards her with his sword drawn. In her head, she can feel Alex's power surging through her body. The power was overwhelming, as it began to build up inside of her. She felt like her body was going to explode at any moment. Suddenly she charged towards the rampaging Akio as he approached her with his sword ready to strike her down. They were now just a few inches away from each other when Akio swung his sword. Raven didn't slow down; she just kept running towards Akio. Then it happened, Tamotsu gasped, he was unable to explain what he was now seeing.

Akio's blade went right through Raven as if she was a ghost. She continued traveling past the blade, straight through Akio catching him totally off guard. Once she made it past him she rematerialized. She jumped into the air spinning then snap kicked Akio across his face, hurling him across the room sending him crashing into the wall. Standing on his feet,

Tamotsu stood with his mouth wide open, but utterly speechless.

Raven stood in the center of the ring, breathing heavily as she slowly returned to her human form. "I did it Mr. Tamotsu!" she replied. She collapsed to the floor, as her body hits the ground two silver bells roll out of her hand. Tamotsu looked over at Alex to see if he saw what Raven did, but to his surprise Alex was also unconscious, stretched out on the floor beside him. Tamotsu just stood there in silence still unable to comprehend what he just witnessed.

EPISODE 8

"ONE TIME AT TRAINING CAMP"

You will not believe the year I've had. Who would have thought I, Raven, the bookworm would be living in a monastery, in Japan learning martial arts and the old ways of the werewolf from a real-life monk. Now I know what you're thinking, "Bitch what happen to you when you passed out?" Well let me just tell you that this was the strangest thing I've ever experienced. When Alex and I were linked our bond was so strong that somehow, I tapped into his abilities and adopted something new of my own. That's what Mr. Tamotsu believes anyway. He also said he has never seen a bond so strong between two people in such a short period of time. Akio thinks it's because we are in love. The thought made me blush, could Alex be in love with me? Am I in love? I mean, he is attractive and he saved my life, not to mention rich and possibly the strongest supernatural creature in existence.

But anyway, after that day we started training me in the martial arts. Every day it was a thousand push-ups, punches, kicks and crunches. Then we ran up and down the mountainside, to and from the village. Ugh, I hated doing all that damn running. My favorite part of the day was weapons training. Mr. Tamotsu showed me a variety of weapons from nun chucks, sai's, and the Katana just to name a few. After Mr. Tamotsu studied my movements, he prescribed the staff as my preferred weapon. Since I was likely to be smaller than the majority of my opponents this would create good distance between them as well as being able to deflect attacks with minimal effort. Mr. Tamotsu had a staff made just for me. It's made of iron just like his, but with some modifications. It can retract so that I can conceal it while in the city and not look like a crazy person. With all the training, learning how to control my new abilities, and even the pack link, there was one thing that was more exciting, more memorable and that is what I want to tell you about.

It all started on a Saturday in the middle of the afternoon. I had just finished training with my iron staff. I wanted to relax and enjoy the rest of the summer day. I went and sat under the shade of a cherry blossom tree in the sand garden, where Alex was putting the final touches on the repairs to the garden. It looked so much better from when he and Tamotsu fought and destroyed it. I sat with my legs crossed trying to appear like I was doing some meditation, but really, I just wanted to watch Alex walk around with his shirt off. He was carrying a large rigid boulder onto the white sand, aligning it with several other large stones. The muscles in his back and arms flexed as he arranged the stones.

Once Alex was pleased with the position of the stones, he moved on grabbing a rake to begin making patterns in the sand to resembled waves in an ocean. Watching Alex gently guide his rake through the soft white sand, I realized what he was doing. He was recreating the island where his home was located off The Amalfi Coast. It took him several hours to finish the football sized sand garden. It was the perfect day, just sitting around under the shade of a cherry blossom tree, enjoying the gentle mountain breeze and a watching shirtless man perform manual labor. All that was missing was cool refreshing drink.

Just when everything seemed right with the world, my good old training buddy and partner in crime came along ruining this perfect moment. Akio rushed over to where I was sitting. He appeared to be excited about something; I could feel it resonating off him. I tried to pretend like I was deep in meditation but he wasn't buying it. He started tapping me on my shoulder and calling my name, "Raven, Raven, Raven…."

I looked at him with one eye closed, "Boy what you want?" I said with an attitude.

"I need your help" Akio replied.

"If it's about training or getting out of chores the answer is no" I replied as I returned to my fake meditation.

"No, no, this is something that will put all this training we've been doing to use. Aren't you tired of sparring with me? Wouldn't you like to see some real action?"

He had my attention now, "I'm listening" I said.

Akio smiled, "For the past couple weeks; there has been talk of people who come or have left our village have gone missing. Some of the villagers have seen abandoned wagons alongside the road and everything. I have reason to believe that vampires have taken residence in the forest abducting villagers to feed on them. So, during the day I've been searching for clues and to make a long story short, I think I found where they have been hiding. As long as they are out there lurking in the shadows, the villagers will never be safe to travel. I'm tired of living in the barrier like prisoners to the night. So, I propose this, how would you like to help eliminate some vampire trash? If we leave now, we can use the light of day to our advantage."

I thought about it for a moment. I had been curious to see how I would do in a real life or death situation. I mean Akio is good to spare with, but just between you and me I've been taking it easy on him during our sparring matches. Honestly, I think I'm ready to challenge Mr. Tamotsu or even Alex.

After a moment of awkward silence, I finally replied, "Fine, but If things get out of hand I'm telling Mr. Tamotsu"

Akio filled with excitement jumped for joy, taking Alex's attentions from raking the white sand garden.

"What are we celebrating?" yelled Alex, from over his shoulder.

Akio and I looked at each other shook like, "What are we going to say?" Suddenly Akio shouted, "Oh I'm just excited Raven agreed to help test out a new technique"

"Oh, ok" replied Alex in a calm unsettling voice as he continued working in the garden. We sighed in relief as we made our way back into the temple. We thought we made it without drawing attention to ourselves when Alex called out to me.

"Raven, you be careful ok. Oh, and Akio if anything happens to her" Alex looked over his shoulder with his eyes burning their sinister ruby red hue. Akio and I shook our heads yes and quickly ran off, leaving Alex to finish his work in the garden. We quickly made our way down the hallway of the temple swiftly passing the sleeping quarters and through the newly rebuilt ceremony room that Alex built by hand. We made our way outside the temple walls past the iron gates of the temple entrance. Once outside the temple gates we made our way down the mountainside through the bamboo forest and into the village. The village was as busy as it was the first day I arrived. This time though the villagers know me now and greeted me as Akio and I pass through.

"Why are we stopping in the village?" I asked Akio.

"Just in case we don't make it back before nightfall I need to let grandfather know to light the front gate torches" replied Akio. He led us into a little shack that served a variety noodles and other authentic Japanese cuisine. The restaurant was just a kitchen with a bar for customers to dine. Sitting at the bar with a whole bottle of sake, was Akio's Grandfather Han.

"Grandfather!" shouted Akio.

Old man Han turned around to greet us in their native language. By now I am familiar with the language so I can understand the conversation.

"Grandfather, we are going outside of the village for a little."

"Ok? Why are you telling me?" replied Han as he took another drink of hot sake.

"Hey, Raven!

"Hello Mr. Han sir" I said with a smile, as he took another sip of sake.

"Just in case we don't make it back before nightfall I want to see if you can light the torches at the front gate"

"What are you two getting into?" asked Han.

"We're just running some training drills grandfather" replied Akio.

Old man Han looked at us for a minute. He contemplated if he was going to believe us or not.

"Ok, you guys have fun" said Han as he poured himself another drink. We exited the restaurant leaving Han to his sake. We made our way to the entrance of the village. As we stood in the entryway of the village Akio turned to me. "Are you ready for this?" Akio asked

"I'm as ready as I'm going to be."

"Good, let's hurry while we still have daylight."

We dashed down the dirt road leaving a cloud of dust in our wake. As we zoomed down the dirt road, a one horse drawn carriage slowly approached the village. We were in a rush so we didn't stop to talk to the man; all we did was wave to the man as we ran past. The driver tilted his hat to greet us. It could have been the excitement of leaving the village but something just didn't feel right. I'm not the smartest in the world but I could have sworn the man was trying to get my attention with his eyes. Or maybe it was the guilt I was feeling for lying to Alex. I shook off the feeling so I could focus on the mission at hand.

The dirt road ran for about a mile leading into the forest. The leaves of the trees were so full and lush, that it blocked out nearly all of the sunlight. Making the forest appear like it was the night time. The air in the forest was much cooler here too. We traveled deep into the forest when I suddenly picked up on a foul stench; it was faint but very noticeable. I stopped dead in my tracks, "Akio, do you smell that?" I whispered. He stopped running, raised his nose into the air as he took a sniff. He inhaled deeply, letting the scent into his nostrils. "Yes, I do" he replied

"The scent is coming from over there" said Akio as he pointed into the forest off of the beaten path"

"You think its vampires or just some dead animal or something?" I asked.

"We won't know unless we go check it out. I mean this is the reason we came into the forest, right?"

I shook my head yes, as we proceeded in the direction of the scent that couldn't only be described as death. The closer we got to the origins of the smell, the stronger the stench. It started to be overbearing for our heightened senses. Personally, I had to cover my nose. After few minutes, we finally arrived to where the funk was emanating from. We stood at the entrance of a cave. Akio stood in front of the cave with a sinister smile on his face. "This has to be the place" he said. He pulled his sword from its sheath then looked into the sky. "We are losing daylight we must hurry"

"I don't know Akio. I'm not sensing the presence of any vampires or any living thing in that cave" I said. He turned back to face me with the look of determination of his face. "They may be hiding their presents from us"

"Which is all the more reason we shouldn't go and investigate; there is no telling how many could be in there. For all we know this could be a trap"

Akio was not trying to hear any of that, and I think I might have upset him because he walked up on me like he was going to hit me but stopped a few inches in front of me. I looked into his eyes and I could see the fury in them.

"Ever since the day I saw Alex-son attacked the village and wiped out an entire clan of vampires, I begged Tamotsu to make me a werewolf like him so I could protect the village from another attack. Now, I have a chance to do that you want me to back do now? If you are too afraid then stay out here, but I'm going in this cave Raven!"

Now I felt bad as I watched Akio march off into the cave alone. "Wait up Akio, I was just saying we should at least have a plan instead of going in blind" I said, trying to sound like I wasn't scared to go into this dark ass cave.

"I do have a plan, find the vampires and kill them all" replied Akio as he continued into the cave.

I followed behind him as he entered the cave. It was pitch black. I reached out with my hands to make sure I didn't run into anything. "I can't see a thing in here" I said as I cautiously made my way through the darkness like a blind person.

"Girl if you don't use your eyes!" barked Akio who was clearly getting annoyed with me.

"Fool, what you...." Before I finished my sentence, I realized what he was saying. "Oooh!" I replied. With a quick blink, I activated my werewolf eyes and instantly I could see. Akio looked back at me shaking his head.

"Well excuse me, I'm still getting the hang of this" I said trying to defend my actions for not knowing we could see in the dark. Akio continued his march through the dark cave.

Its interior was no different from any other cave; full of rocks and dirt everywhere, I even had those stones hanging from the ceiling that looked like rock icicles. The air in the cave was thick and humid, not to mention the horrible smell of death lingered. We followed the scent which leads us downward into the cave. The further down we went the stronger the smell became until we came to a large opening where we found what we were looking for. It was a horrific sight. I could feel Akio becoming enraged as he let out a low audible growl that echoed through the cave. I covered my mouth as I gasped at the sight laid out before us.

Scattered all over the cave floor like dirty laundry was the lifeless bodies of the missing villagers and travelers from the surrounding areas.

"I knew it" said Akio

"There are sooooo! How long has this been going on?" I asked.

"I'm not sure, but it ends tonight" replied Akio. He kneeled down to inspect one of the bodies. Just as he suspected, the victim was drained of her blood.

As he was examining the bodies, I continued investigating the cave to see if there were more bodies. I followed a trail of bodies that lead me around to another part of the cave. Everything seemed fine, until I found something that looked out of place. There were marks on the ground that looked like someone or something was dragged, but with a closer look it wasn't drag marks, but wheel marks. When I realized what I found I screamed for Akio. He came running, weapon in hand.

"What is it!?" asked Akio

"Look!" I said, pointing at the ground.

"Ok?"

"They're tracks made from a wagon!"

I could see in his eyes he realized what I was getting at. Before we could get another would out, the sound of a wolf's howl could be heard in the distance.

"Who the hell was that? I asked. It wasn't Mr. Tamotsu or Alex, it sounded too artificial.

"Oh no!" said Akio. He looked terrified.

"What is it?" I asked. By now I was getting worried.

"That was grandfather. We had a horn made for him that he could use to get in contact with me or Mr. Tamotsu in the event he ever got into trouble. We have to get back to the village immediately"

Back at the village

The sun began to set on the small village under the mountain, as Old man Han finished his last cup of sake. He downs the drink, titling his head back, allowing the alcohol to rush down his throat quickly. He slams the cup on the counter, then exits the restaurant. He slowly makes his way to his post located at the back of the village as the villagers were getting ready to settle into their homes for the evening.

Han finally reached his post. He reached into his pocket and pulls out a box of matches. He slid open the box, pulling out a single match then strikes the match across his chin. The match ignited, then Han pulls out another match lighting it with the first match then throwing a match in each of the two torches. The flames irrupted with a flash of light as a dim aurora began to travel the length of the village then stopping half way. Once the torches were lit, Han made his way to the front of the village to ignite the last two torches. On his way to the front, he noticed that night had fallen and his grandson has not returned with Raven. He picked up the pace hobbling through the village market place as quickly as he could.

When he came to the end of the market place he noticed a man resting against his one horse drawn buggy. Han didn't think anything of it; the man could just be a merchant resting before leaving the village. The man got to his feet and walked to the back of the buggy. He pulled the cover off revealing four black coffins. Han started to feel a chill in the air, the same chill he use to get before a battle.

"The sun has set, you can come out now" replied the man as he spoke directly to the coffins. Slowly, one by one the coffins began to open. Emerging from the coffins were four Asian men; they were dressed in modern city clothes. Han stood still in his tracks as his worst nightmare became a reality right before his eyes. He thought he would die before vampires breached the village barrier.

The four men leaped from the buggy onto the ground. They stretched their limbs as if they had been cooped up in their coffins for hours.

"Didn't I tell you boys this place existed!" replied the shortest of the four men.

"I can't believe people still live like this in the twenty first century" said another of the vampires as he adjusted his glasses.

"I know. By the time anyone stumbles across this place we will be back in Tokyo in the comforts of our homes" said the shortest one of the group.

Han slowly reached for a brass horn that was shaped like a wolf's head with its mouth open. He gently unlatched it from his waist, trying not to draw attention to himself but it was too late. One of the vampires; the largest one of the group spotted Han standing in the middle of the market place.

"Looks like we've been spotted boys" said the larger muscular vampire.

The others turned to look in Hans's direction, with their emerald green eyes focused on him.

"Oh look, the little old man is dressed in armor, and look at his cute little straw hat" said the muscular vampire.

The four-vampire burst into hysterical laughter. "What do you think you're going to do to us old man?" asked the short vampire.

Without hesitation, Han put the brass horn to his lips and blew into it with all his might. The horn created the sound of a wolf's howl that echoed through the night sky. The villagers heard the sound and immediately began to rush to their homes screaming and panicking.

"Great! Now we lost the element of surprise" said the short vampire. "Hurry and catch as many as you can before they enter their homes. Once they inside we won't be able to get inside without being invited"

"You guys go ahead; I'll deal with the old man" said the muscular vampire as cracked his knuckles."

"Ok suit yourself" said the vampire as he adjusted his glasses before dashing off after the villagers. The short vampire and the other vampire followed after him, leaving the muscular vampire to deal with Han.

"We weren't expecting someone to be guarding this village, we thought it would be an easy feast, but this is a pleasant surprise" said the muscle-bound vampire. "My name is Takeshi, I think it's only right I tell you my name before I take your life old man."

Han knew he was no match for this vampire, but he had a trump card. Hanging from his waist next to the brass wolf horn, was a calabash-shaped gourd with a bird on it filled with a mysterious liquid. He grabbed the gourd to drink the contents inside.

"Oh, having a finally drink before you die?"

"You sure do talk a lot, are you going to kill me or what? I'm not getting any younger" replied Han with an old raspy voice. Han finished the last of the contents in the gourd then tossed it away. Han began to sway back and forth as he flashed his one tooth smile, as he waved to Takeshi to come after him.

"As you wish old man" smiled Takeshi as he charged towards Han expecting to end him quickly. Han just stood there swaying like a buoy in the ocean. Takeshi was inches away from Han reaching out to rip his heart, but at the last second Han rolled out the way, spinning off of Takeshi's body using his momentum to position himself behind Takeshi, pulling a wooden stake from his pocket then plunging it into Takeshi's back Takeshi screamed in pain as the stake punctured his heart. Han finished Takeshi off by kicking the stake through his back and out his chest.

The emerald light left Takeshi's eyes as his lifeless body collapse to the ground. The other three vampires came rushing back to where Han and Takeshi fought. They were hoping to find their friend feasting on the blood of the old man, but instead found their brethren lying lifeless on the ground and next to him the old man. He lied on the ground with his head propped up in his hand.

"I was wondering when you three would get here" replied Han with a smirk on his face.

"You will pay for this old man" shouted the short vampire.

Han smiled then suddenly burped up flames. "Oh no" Han thought to himself. 'It's starting already; I need to end this quickly"

"What the hell is going on" said the short vampire.

"You are about to find out" replied Han as he leaped to his feet, stumbling into his drunken fighting stance. The three vampires started walking towards Han, when from behind Han came a loud thunderous sound. When Han turned around, he saw his grandson Akio standing in the gateway of the village roaring with his eyes glowing their luminous yellow. Standing behind he was Raven lighting the torches, sealing them inside the village. Han smiles, then looked back at the vampires, "I would like for you to meet my werewolf grandson and his American friend Raven, also a werewolf" smirked Han. His smile was wiped from his face when he burped up more flames.

Akio saw this and ran to his grandfather's side, with Raven following close behind him.

"Grandfather please tell me you didn't do it", asked a concerned Akio.

"I had to grandson; I rather die fighting, than to let these demons harm the people of this village."

"What are you guys talking about?" asked Raven

"Grandfather drank the Elixir of the Phoenix"

"The what?" Raven replied.

"The Elixir gives the user incredible strength and speed at the cost of their life"

Raven covered her mouth in shock." Oh no, she replied.

"It's ok, I've lived a long life, dying in battle is an honorable death" said Han

Don't worry you will be joining him some" said the short vampire. He snapped his fingers and without hesitation the two vampires he was with attacked. The vampire with the glasses attack Han forcing him back into the market place. The other vampire attacked Akio leading him away, leaving Raven to deal with the short vampire.

"I've never killed an American werewolf before, this will be a pleasure" replied the arrogant short vampire.

"Don't underestimate me little man" said Raven.

"What did you say you American bitch!? You will pay for that! Before I kill you, I'll have my way with you"

"Whatever you say, little China man!"

Enraged the vampire shouted, "I'm not Chinese!" His eyes burned bright emerald green as he charged Raven…

Back at the Mountain Temple

Pacing back and forth in the newly remodeled ceremony hall, Alex eagerly awaited the return of Raven. "She has been gone for hours with Akio. The sun has finally set meaning the village below will be lighting the torches making it impossible for Akio and Raven to return to the temple tonight", Alex thought to himself.

As Alex continues to pace the ceremony hall, Tamotsu entered the room.

"Why are you pacing?" asked Tamotsu.

"Akio came and took Raven into the village earlier today and they haven't returned. I have a bad feeling about this" said Alex.

"They will be fine; the village is the safest place for them besides the temple. I'm sure they are…." Tamotsu was interrupted by the unexpected sound of a wolf's howl.

"I fucking knew it! I knew they were up to something. Who was that?" shouted Alex

Dread came over Tamotsu's face as the wolf's howl echoed through the evening sky. "That was old man Han's wolf horn, the barrier has been breached.

Alex rushed to the back of the ceremony room, snatching his sword that sat peacefully on its display then made a mad dash out of the temple. He still wore his magical iron gauntlets, so he was unable to teleport. He quickly made it outside past the temple gates. Instead of taking the path down the mountainside, Alex ran towards the edge of the mountain cliff and without hesitation leaped off the mountain. Free falling towards the bamboo forest, flipping and twisting his body like an Olympic swimmer. Quickly approaching the bamboo he used his werewolf claws to grab the bamboo to slow his descent. He was coming in too fast to slow down completely due to the weights he was too heavy. He hit the ground with a thunderous sound creating a creator where he landed. Alex forgot he weighed 2 tons while wearing his magical gauntlets. Alex sprinted off towards the village post haste. Tamotsu landed moments after Alex, following after him. They were a mile away from the village, using their superior speed they cleared the distance in an instance. Once they reached the gates they saw the torches were light, causing

Alex to come to a screeching haul. Standing in front the village gate, Alex examined the barrier. He slowly reached out with his hand. The barrier rippled as his hand touched the invisible barrier that prevented him from entering the village. A heat washed over Alex as he grew angry. Filled with rage Alex roared, as he punching the barrier. The force from his punch caused a loud booming sound. The barrier rippled like a pebble being tossed in body of water.

"Fucking barrier!" shouted Alex

"Looks like we are too late" replied Tamotsu calmly as he walked up.

"Is there another way into the village?" asked Alex.

Tamotsu shook his head no.

"Then how are we supposed to get into the village to help?" shouted Alex.

"Clear your mind Alex-son, the answer will come to you" replied Tamotsu.

Frustrated, Alex took a deep breath, then sat on the ground crossing his legs. Tamotsu smiled as he watched his oldest student and longtime friend finally understanding what he has tried to teach him for the past one hundred years; patience.

Tamotsu sat next to Alex. "Now let's concentrate and see what they have gotten there selves into"

Spinning and dodging attacks, Han defended himself against the vampire wearing glasses. The vampire threw a series of punches that Han evades with fluid motions. With the Elixir of the Phoenix now in his system, he was now able to keep up with his vampire attacker. After evading the vampire's attacks, Han goes on the attack. Moving like a drunken sailor he threw punches and kicks from odd angles making it difficult for the vampire to block. Han went low with a series of sweeps that knocked the vampire hard on his back. Han then rolled on the ground towards the vampire then dropped an elbow on his chest with enough force that shattered several of the vampire's ribs. The vampire screamed in agony as he pushed Han off of him, sending him hurling into a nearby shop destroying it in an instant. The debris that now covered Hans's body erupted into a ball of flames. Han emerged from the flames unharmed as he continued coughing up balls fire.

"I don't have much time left, I need to make my move now" Han thought to himself. Han charged his spectacle wearing opponent, tackling him to the ground. Han proceeded to put the vampire in a submission hold that the vampire was unable to free himself.

"Release me you disgusting old man" grunted the vampire as he desperately tried to break free of Han's mighty grip.

"This is where you die vampire" Han whispered in the vampire's ear, hoping to get one last glimpse of his grandson. Han knew he was out of time. His eyes began to tear up as he felt his insides boil.

"Farewell grandson" replied Han as he combusted into flames. The vampire's screams of agony filled the air, grabbing everyone's attention.

Akio stopped fighting as he saw his grandfather go up in a ball of flames. He kicked the vampire he was fighting sending him crashing to a wall. Akio ran towards his grandfather to put out the flames. He was a mere inches away from where his grandfather and the vampire burned alive when he was kicked in the side of the head by the very vampire he was fighting moments before. The kick sent Akio's body hurling into the noodle shack, his grandfather loved. The building exploded as Akio's body smashed into it causing the surrounding shacks to crumble leaving Akio unconscious, buried under the debris.

That left Raven alone to deal with two vampires alone. She ran over to see if Akio was ok, but before she could get close to him, the short vampire she was fighting appeared in front of her, followed by the vampire that kicked Akio unconscious.

"I'm very impressed with your skills American, but it appears you are now alone to fight my friend and me. So, before I kill you I'll tell you my name…."

As the short Japanese vampire gave his bad guy monologue, a voice called out to her. She looked around but didn't see anyone but the two vampires. The voice called to her again, this time she knew who it was. She recognized that smooth baritone voice anywhere. It was Alex calling to her. He must be performing the battle meditation. She cleared her mind, closing her eyes and took a deep breath. When she opened her eyes, she was no longer in the village but standing in the same place the last time Alex connected with her through their pack link.

Surrounded by white, hazy nothingness, Alex sat atop a black fluffy storm cloud, as random lightning strikes flickered throughout the cloud. She rushed over to him.

"Alex, I need your help" she said in a panic. "Four vampires have entered the village. Grandpa Han killed two of them but he's…. and now Akio is unconscious and I'm alone with these two vampires."

Alex got up from his cloud, making his way to Raven. He pulled her close to her hug.

"I was worried sick about you, I'm glad you're ok" he said as he held her tight. "I'm sorry to hear about Old man Han and Akio, but you are not alone"

"Are you inside the village?" Raven asked desperately.

"No, Tamotsu and I didn't make in time before the torches were lit, we are sitting in front of the barrier."

"Ok, can you have Mr. Tamotsu take these bracelets off me?"

Alex released Raven, "He physically has to do that. I was thinking we give the power transfer thing another try" Alex suggested.

"Are you crazy? Last time we did that we were completely drained, and it only lasted for like a whole minute. Plus, I don't like the way it makes me feel. It's like I'm not myself, like I'm somebody else" Raven argued.

"We're a lot stronger now, and it's really our only option"

Raven thought it over. She was barely keeping up with the one vampire she was fighting and now she has two opponents.

"Fine, I'm going to die anyway if I don't do something"

"Good," replied Alex as he took his seat back on his storm cloud. A white cloud formed in front of Alex for Raven "Now let's kick some vampire ass!" smiled Alex as he winked at Raven before going into his trance.

Raven found herself back in the village as the short vampire was still monologe'in

"Oh, my god!" Raven shouted "Are we going to fight or are you going to talk me to death"

The vampires were shocked by her sudden outburst. Raven cracked her knuckles, "You killed grandpa Han, hurt my friend and tried to hurt the peaceful people of this village! Little china man, your ass is mine!" said Raven taking a more aggressive fighting stance.

The short vampire became instantly furious, lunging at Raven. She pivoted allowing the vampire to pass her. The second vampire joined the fight. Raven blocked and dodged both of their attacks almost effortlessly.

"How did you suddenly get so strong?" asked the short vampire.

"Ugh, more talking, here let me close that mouth for you" said Raven, leaping into the air kicking the short vampire in the face. The force of her kick snapped his neck as his body spun in midair, then crashing to the ground. The other vampire charged Raven, as she landed on her feet she ducked down into a spinning sweep kick knocking the vampire flat on his face. Then she leaped into the air flipping and twirling. When she reached the height of jump she unleashed her claws speeding back towards the vampire who lied helplessly on the ground. Before the vampire could react, Raven crashed on top of him, sinking her claws into his chest, snatching out his heart out.

She stood up then kicked the vampire's lifeless body across the ground. "That was easier than I thought" Raven said, walking towards the short vampire, who lied unconscious on the ground. She was just a few steps away from the vampire when his neck snapped back into place.

"You fucking bitch, you tried to kill me!" said little china man which Raven coined him; picking himself up off the ground.

Tilting her head like a curious little puppy, starring with her one red eye, and one yellow eye.

"So, stake to the heart, or ripping your heart out is the only way to kill you vampires" replied Raven.

Little China man walked over to one of the destroyed merchant shops, pulling a sword from the ruble.

"This isn't silver but I'll use this to cut you head off, you can't heal from that" said little china man.

"Cut my head off? You can try little China man" smirked Raven as she removed her iron staff from its holster on the small of her back. She pressed down on the staff causing the staff to extend, then twirled it around her into her fighting stance. Little China man charged after Raven, slashing at her as she twirled her iron staff deflection his attacks effortlessly

"I expected more from my first encounter with a vampire, I'm so underwhelmed" said Raven.

Little China man became furious as he continued his assault. His every attempt was foiled by the impenetrable barrier Raven created by twirling her iron staff.

"Ok, my turn," said Raven. She twisted the center of the staff and from tip of her staff; a blade appeared turning her staff into a spear. Going on the offense she swung the spear high and low causing the vampire to backpedal into a retreat. Raven continued her assault on the vampire she called little china man. With the combined powers of Alex and her own, the vampire was no match for her. She was too fast for him; it was like she was attacking him from multiple angles all at once. Unable to horde off her attacks, the vampire was hit in the legs causing him to fall to one knee. She then spun the spear around her body building up momentum then with one final slash she severed his head.

The vampire she called little china man, was dead. She kicked his headless body over as it toppled to the ground. Raven looked around searching for another opponent. "There has to be someone else I can fight, that was disappointing" she thought to herself. She started to grin as she thought of a sinister idea. Without hesitation, she sprinted to the back of the village where the gates leading to the temple were. Standing in front of the gate as the torches burned. Raven stood staring at her next opponent.

"Raven, where is Akio?" asked Tamotsu.

"He was taken out by one of the vampires, but don't worry I've eliminated the vampire threat in the village" said Raven staring at Alex with her mismatched eyes.

"Is he dead?" asked Tamotsu concerned about his beta.

"I don't know I didn't stop to check" replied Raven, frowning her face at her master.

She reached out with her hand as the barrier rippled under her palm. She then looked at the two lit torches. "So, this is why you are unable to enter the village. Well I'll just take care of that.

"Raven what are you doing?" replied Tamotsu.

"He is unfit to be my Alpha, if I kill him, I'll become the new Alpha and this power will be mine"

Tamotsu finally understood why Alex was able to control his Full transformation while in battle meditation. Somehow he was channeling it throw Raven. Now it has fused with her, making her different as if someone else was inside her head. Tamotsu attempted to wake Alex up but he was lost in his trance. He continued to try breaking Alex's concentration but he was unsuccessful. Raven took her spear swung it at the flames of the torches. The gust of wind she created extinguished the flames, lowering the barrier.

"I'll make this quick" said Raven as she raised her spear to throw it at a defenseless Alex.

"Raven, don't make me do this" pleaded Tamotsu as he stood between Raven and Alex with arms extended.

"Move or I'll go straight through you" Raven replied in a cold-hearted voice.

"Do what you must"

"My pleasure" Raven lunged her spear at Tamotsu. Her spear plunged into the ground. Raven was shocked to find Tamotsu and Alex was no longer in front of her. Standing behind her with his arms still extended was Mr. Tamotsu with his eyes closed. When he opened his eyes, he was now behind Raven. He let out a sigh of relief.

"Cutting it close don't you think" replied Tamotsu.

Standing up from his sitting position was Alex, "Sorry about that, our connection had me in a deep trance. What's going on?" asked Alex.

"It seems the reason you are able to transform without going berserk is because Raven was taking on the burden for you. But now it looks your suppressed rage has manifested itself in Raven and wants to kill you and take your Alpha powers for its own.

"I can't believe I did this to her" replied Alex.

Raven started walking towards Tamotsu and Alex. "Alexander, I challenge you for the right to be Alpha, do you accept my challenge or are you going to hide behind Tamotsu?" said Raven twirling her weapon.

"She is not herself Alex" mentioned Tamotsu

"I know, but this is all my fault. If I would have handled my issues sooner, she wouldn't be possessed by my corruption. I'll handle this and save Raven. Whatever happens do not interfere"

"Ok, but before you go, allow me" Tamotsu waved his hands over Alex's iron gauntlets, releasing him from the burden of carrying the weight of two ton.

"This should help you move more freely. She has some of your Alpha powers look at her left eye."

Alex looked at her staring at them with her head tilted as her left eye burned ruby red.

"I see" replied Alex. "I'll make sure I stay on my toes" Alex placed his hand on Tamotsu's shoulder. In the blink of an eye Tamotsu and Alex were standing at the top of the mountain just outside of the temple gates.

"Alex-son, what are you doing?"

"Ensuring you don't get in the way old friend."

Before Tamotsu could say another word, Alex was gone, leaving Tamotsu standing at the temple gates alone.

Alex reappeared in the village, where Raven waited.

"I thought you chicken out." Raven said in a sarcastic tone.

Alex didn't respond, as he made his way to the torches. He extended his claws and scratched the metal of the torches creating sparks, reigniting the flames.

"I accept your challenge. You want to be Alpha then come get it" said Alex as his eyes change color; one eye turning red while the other was yellow.

"So, you're not a coward after all Alexander" said Raven as she crouched into her fighting stance.

"What did you call me?" asked Alex.

"I thought you would have realized by now, Alexander"

Something about the way she called him Alexander made him feel nostalgic. It finally dawned on him as he stared at Raven with wide eyes.

She smiled at him, "That's right. I told you it was going to be either her or me but you didn't listen"

"Isis? It's been you controlling Raven this whole time?" said Alex.

"Yes, my love… Sorry it has to be this way, but you will never reach your full potential unless you deal with this now. You have two choices kill me or I kill you then I kill her"

"Don't do this"

"No more talking" Isis, who now possesses Raven's body, plunged her spear into the ground as she charged Alex. She throws a series of punches that he dodges. Alex countered her attacks with his own flurry of punches followed by a roundhouse kick that Isis barely evades.

"This body is a little too slow" replied Isis. "It must be these hideous bangles. I can fix that." Isis, closed her eyes, then suddenly she dematerialized. The bangles and her shin guards fell to the ground. She re-materialized, rubbing her wrist. "Oh, that's much better. "Now let's see what this beta can really do"

The possessed Raven now moved with incredible speed that caught Alex off guard. She instantly appeared in front of him throwing punches, that Alex was forced to block. She jumped in the air throwing a spinning roundhouse kick. The power behind her kicks forced Alex to stumble back. Continuing her vicious assault, she landed on the ground instantly crouching into a sweep kick, clipping Alex's heel, sending him to the ground.

"I don't think you're taking me seriously Alexander."

"Isis, let her go, you don't have to do this."

"Yes, I do. If you are going to challenge a blue blood you are going to need full control of all your powers. You can't be some raging beast,that will get you killed. The only way you're going to defeat me is with your final form."

"Please, if I do, I'll kill you and her" pleaded Alex.

Isis ignored his request as she cause Raven to turn into her final form. "Oh, this is exhilarating. I'm going to enjoy this, my love" replied Isis. Isis backflips back to where she planted her spear. She snatches it out of the ground, giving it a twirl in between her fingers.

Alex got to his feet, dusting off his all black-monk robes. "I guess you leave me no choice, I said I would be the Alpha Raven needs me to be" replied Alex. With sadness in his eyes, Alex took his second form. Isis shook her head; disappointed Alex still wouldn't go into his final form. Isis propelled Ravens body towards Alex, spinning and twirling her iron spear, poking and slashing at Alex. Holding his sword in its sheath with his left hand, Alex dodged Isis attacks, trying desperately to avoid harming her.

But now with her being possessed by the vampire princess and free of the training weights, Raven was as strong as Master Tamotsu if not stronger. Isis continued her assault, controlling Ravens every move like she was a deadly puppet. Alex continued to evade and block her attacks. Tamotsu finally made it back to the village. He stood at the entrance of the village unable to enter to aid his friend. All he could do is spectate from behind the magical barrier.

Refusing to fight, Alex was being tossed around the village as Isis beat him with the iron spear. The clanging sound of the iron spear colliding with his body echoed through the evening sky. Isis hit Alex into a nearby building causing it to shatter as debris from the collapsing building fell on top of Alex burying him.

"It seems like you rather have this poor young wolf die, instead of letting me go. I guess this is the end for her" said Isis.

Controlling Ravens body, Isis turned the spear towards herself with the tip of the blade pressed on Raven's chest. Tamotsu stood at the barrier as he watched helplessly. To him it looked like Raven was going to committee suicide. He was not aware she was being controlled by Isis.

Isis raised the spear in the air preparing to stab herself in the heart when a loud screeching roar stopped her dead in her tracks. From the ruble emerged Alex in his final form. The whites of his eyes were jet black while his pupils burned their bright ruby red. Alex flesh was now covered in black fur similar to that of a black panther. .His face, chest and abdominal area were bare flesh of a dark greyish hue.

"Finally, you take me seriously…" in the blink of an eye, Alex snatched the spear from Raven's hand.

"I begged you not to do this, but you wouldn't listen. Then you go and try to harm Raven. As her Alpha, that is unforgivable. Princess Isis, last of the Royal Clan, today is the day you die."

Alex lets out a roar that could be heard in the heavens. It was like the sound of a lion mixed with a T-Rex.

"That's more like it Alexander" replied Isis as she charged Alex unleashing a barrage of punches that Alex easily avoided. He countered her last attack with a single punch to her stomach that dropped her to her knees knocking her out of her werewolf form.

Isis clutched her stomach gasping for air.

"Like I said Isis, I will not allow you to harm Raven"

Isis smirked, "Good now finish me"

Banging on the barrier, desperately trying to get Alex's attention Tamotsu shouted, "Don't do it Alex-son! Stop this, you're stronger than this!" Tamotsu continued but his cries fell on deaf ears, leaving Tamotsu to be nothing more than a witness to the slaughter of his new student.

Alex walked up to Isis, grabbing her by the neck lifting her into the air. Isis gasped for air as Alex clasped his claws around her throat.

"I'll never let anything happen to Raven, not even let you harm her. Good bye my love.

A tear fell from her face as she faced an inevitable death. She closed her eyes awaiting the end. She felt a sharp pain in her shoulder. She opened her eyes to find Alex sinking his teeth into her shoulder. Then he released his grip on Raven letting her body fall to the ground.

"What was that!?I said you had to kill me Alexander" Shouted Isis, coughing as she tried to catch her breath.

Alex looked down at Isis who occupied Ravens body with a disgusted look on his face.

"That is exactly what I've done. You are a vampire spirit in a werewolf body, and what is the cruelest way to kill a vampire besides sunlight?"

Isis thought for a second as everything started to make since.

"Very clever Alexander, using your werewolf venom to kill me, without harming your precious beta. Look at yourself, you have total control over your final form" said Isis as she was beginning to lose consciousness. She collapsed to the ground, as the werewolf venom eliminated the presents of Isis inside Raven. Alex kneeled down to Raven cradling her in his arms.

"It looks like you are becoming the Alpha I knew you would be my love" said Isis as she caressed Alex's face. Slowly Alex began to return to his normal form.

"Thank you, for believing in me, I will always love you, but you are right. I have to let you go" whispered Alex.

Isis smiled as she slipped back into eternal darkness. Alex held Raven in his arms as the scene reminded him of that fateful night a hundred and fifty years ago, when he held Isis the same way. As she rested peacefully in Alex's arms, Raven began to move as she slowly opened her eyes.

"Ugh, I think I met your ex-girlfriend, she seemed nice" replied Raven.

Alex smiled, "Everything is fine now, I'm glad you back to normal" said Alex.

"Next time, you want to share your issues let's talk them out first instead of sharing them LITERALLY!" said Raven.

Alex laughed, "From now on, if I have a problem I'll try using my words" snickered Alex.

"Good, now excuse me I need to rest" mumbled Raven as she passed out from exhaustion.

Alex just sat there holding Raven, surrounded by destruction as the sun began to rise, "ironic how history has a funny way of repeating itself" he thought

As the sun rose on the little village under the mountain, the barrier began to dissolve as the sunlight washed over the village. Once the barrier was down, Tamotsu rushed over to where Alex was sitting, holding Raven in his arms.

"Alex-son, what in the world just happened?"

"Long story short, my suppressed, issues about the loss of the princess manifested itself in Raven during our link allowing it to possess Raven" explained Alex.

"Is she….?"

"No, she is resting"

In the distance, movement could be heard under the debris of one the fallen buildings.

"Oh my god, Akio" said Tamotsu running to help his beta from under the rubble. Lifting the debris off of Akio, Tamotsu helped him to his feet.

"What happened?" asked Akio, still disoriented.

"Are you ok…?" replied Tamotsu

"I'm fine I……. no, grandfather!"

In the middle of the village market place was a large pile of ashes where Akio's grandfather, Han scarified himself to protect the villagers, Raven and his grandson. Akio's eyes began to swell with tears, his heart filled with sorrow at the thought of his grandfather's sacrifice. Tamotsu and Akio stood in silence as they honored their fallen when a spark flickered within the ashes. Akio thought it was the light reflecting off the tears in his eyes. He wiped his eyes using the sleeve of his tonic, returning his gaze at the remains of his grandfather. As he was about to accept what he saw as just his mind playing tricks on him, the pile of ashes erupted into a ball of flames.

"Sensei am I going crazy" replied Akio.

"No, I see it too my apprentice and I have no idea what is going on."

Alex; carrying Raven in his arms, made his way over to where they were standing, "Do you guys feel…… What the hell?" replied Alex as he watched the ashes burning wildly? From the flames, the three watched as a hand reached out from the flames. Tamotsu, Akio and Alex gasped as someone emerged from the raging blaze

"What type of freaky shit is going on here?" replied Alex.

The flames died as suddenly as they started. Standing in the center of the ashes dressed in all white monk robes was a younger looking Han. He appeared to be in his early fifties with streaks of gray in his beard, and hair.

The silence was broken as Akio said softly, "Grandfather?"

"Grandson!" replied Han.

Akio rushed into his grandfather's arms, squeezing him tightly.

"How is this possible? Are you really here?" questioned Akio, still unable to fathom the idea of his once dead grandfather now resurrected.

"Yes, it's definitely me Akio. I heard stories that the elixir could bring you back to life, but everyone was too afraid to test that theory. I'm just glad it was true.

"Me too, grandfather, me too"

EPISODE 9

"BACK TO BUSINESS"

Several weeks after the attack on the village, Tamotsu, Alex, Raven, Akio and Old man Han all were gathered in the ceremony hall of the temple. Alex and Raven have completed their training and are now getting ready to go back home to America.

"You two have come a long way, since you arrived here a year ago. Take what you have learned here, to keep yourself safe. I don't know what you two have gotten into but be careful" said Tamotsu.

"Don't worry old friend, we will be extra cautious" smiled Alex

"I'll make sure he stays out of trouble Mr. Tamotsu" said Raven as she gave her teacher a hug.

"What do you guys plan to do now?" Alex asked.

"Well now that the Elixir is gone, I want to find the recipe to create more for the next generation." replied Han

"You're leaving the village?" replied Alex

"I'm going with him too" said Akio

"Then, who will protect the village and light the torches?" replied Raven.

"After the incident in the village, I have gained a few new students who want help protect the village" replied Tamotsu.

"Sounds like you will be busy after all old friend" replied Alex.

"If you guys get into trouble, don't hesitate to come get us "replied Tamotsu

"Yeah, I've always wanted to go to America" said Akio

"I'll keep that in mind. Well, we're off" said Alex, shaking the hands of his friends.

Alex took Raven by the hand as they stood holding there belongs.

"See you guys later!" said Alex, and in a blink of an eye they vanished.

They reappeared seconds later in the living room of Alex's island estate.

"Home, sweet, home" replied Alex as he inhaled the island air.

"Excuse me, but I've waiting forever for modern plumbing" said Raven dropping her bags as she ran for the bathroom. After an hour in the bathroom, Raven finally returned back downstairs in her red bathrobe feeling refreshed. She finds Alex in the kitchen making him a sandwich.

"I feel so much better. So, what's next?"

"Well I was thinking it would be a shame for you to go through all that training and not put it to good use. How do you feel about joining a hunter's guild?" asked Alex.

"What is that?" question Raven.

"They hunt down supernatural beings that harm humans or even other super naturals. When a bounty is placed on someone's head, hunters can go and take care of that particular job. You can make some good money while you're at it."

"That sounds exciting!"

"Good, but first things first, we need to get you some gear if you plan on joining a guild. I have an old friend we can pay a visit."

Raven was filled with excitement as she ran upstairs to get dressed. "I'll be right back let me get dressed" Raven shouted from the upstairs bedroom. She came back dressed and ready to go.

"Ok, I'm ready"

"That was faster than I thought, you must be really eager to get your revenge"

"After Japan, I'm ready to get out here; I still haven't really used my own powers yet, so I'm just excited"

"You're starting to sound more and more like me" said Alex as they exchanged smiles. "Well let's get going"

Alex walked up on Raven, placing his around her waist pulling her close to him. Looking into her eyes, "Hold on" Alex said softly as they vanished into thin air.

Sitting behind the counter of a local pawn shop, Harvey; the owner of the shop was polishing an elegant silver dagger, when two young men enter his establishment carrying electronics. Dressed in skinny jeans and a hoodie, one of the young men dropped his questionable merchandise on the counter while his friend stood close to the door.

"What up old man, how much can I get for these?" asked the young man.

Harvey examined the items given to him, "Where's the chargers to these laptops?"

"Oh, I must have left those at home"

Harvey knew the items were clearly stolen goods. "Without the chargers, I can't offer you anything" said Harvey, returning the young man his items.

"Come on old man, this shit is basically brand new"

"I told you this was a bad idea" replied the young man standing at the door.

Harvey noticed the young man was wearing a necklace and watch that appeared to be made of silver.

"I'll give you a hundred and fifty dollars for your friend's jewelry" Harvey proposed.

The young man standing by the door looked at Harvey, offended by the offer. "Oh, hell naw, I'm not giving up my shit!"

"Come on man" his friend pleaded.

"Not gonna be able to do it" replied his friend, still posted by the door.

"Well it looks like our business is done here" replied Harvey as he returned his attention to cleaning and sharpening his silver dagger. The two young men exchange a look, and without saying a word the young man standing by the entrance pulled a gun from his waist. The young man who was at the counter shrugged his shoulders as he followed suit

"I didn't want to have to do this!" said the young man standing at the counter.

With a gun pointed to his head, Harvey never looked away from cleaning his silver dagger.

"I'm going to make you one last offer. Either you take the 150.00 for the jewelry, or I take the jewelry, these stolen goods and for my inconvenience take those guns too" said Harvey in a calm tone.

The two-young men burst into laughter. "Maaaaan fu…." Before the young man at the counter could finish his sentence Harvey sprang into action, ripping the gun out the young man's hand. He reached up grabbing the boy by the back of his head then slamming it on the counter cracking the glass, then dragging him across the counter using him as a human shield as he points the gun at the youngster standing at the door. Everything happened so fast that the young man couldn't react in time.

"Take the jewelry off, before I shoot you and take the shit!" shouted Harvey.

"Just give the old nigga that cheap ass jewelry!" begged the boy as blood ran from the gash over his left eye.

The boy thought about it for a second, and then lowered his gun so he could remove his jewelry.

"Wise decision" replied Harvey as he kept the gun pointed at the boy. "Drop the jewelry right there and the gun right there on the floor, slowly" Harvey instructed.

The boy did as he was told laying both the gun and his jewelry on the floor at his feet.

"Good, now kick it over to me"

The boy kicked the items towards the counter.

"Alright now step back"

The young man walked slowly back towards the door, still facing Harvey. Once he was at the door Harvey slowly released his grip on his hostage, who gasped for air as he was freed.

"Now get the hell out my shop!" demanded Harvey, gun still pointed at the boys.

"This ain't over old man" replied the boys as they exited the store.

"You know where to find me with your punk ass" shouted Harvey. He locked the door after the boys left the shop, then turned off the neon light open sign. He gathered the stolen items off the floor along with the gun as he made his way back behind the counter. Harvey took his items through the "employee only door", which lead downstairs.

Once down in the basement, it was like he stepped into a whole different world. Upstairs looked like your typical pawnshop, with everything from electronics down to firearm encased in glass topped cabinets. Downstairs on the other hand looked like a sophisticated weapons shop. The walls were filled with a variety of larger firearms, weapons that looked like they packed a punch. In the center of the room was another display case filled with smaller firearms and various hand grenades. The case next to it held swords and daggers, all with exquisite craftsmanship.

In a corner in the back of the basement, a young man was sitting at a workstation. He was focused on his latest invention as he tinkered with the mechanics of the device. The young man didn't hear Harvey enter the shop as he had his headphones on blasting his music.

"Junior?!" shouted Harvey, but his son didn't respond. Taking the items, he had, Harvey dropped them on Junior's working station. Junior jumped out his seat terrified.

"Jesus pop! You scared the crap out of me!" said Junior, placing his hand over his heart.

"Maybe if you turn down that loud music, you could hear someone coming"

"You right pop. So, what you got there?" asked Junior as he fixed his glasses on his face.

"These young punks tried to sell this stolen shit. Look, they didn't even bring the damn charges with them" replied Harvey growing frustrated.

"It's cool pop, I'll take these and put them with the rest of the "donations" said Junior with chuckle.

As Junior put the stolen items in a bin next to his workstation, Harvey examined his son's most recent invention.

"So, what you working on?" asked Harvey intrigued by this futuristic weapon.

"Oh that? Pop, I call it the Sunburst. It's a highly modified sawed-off shotgun that generates an enormous burst of UV light. This baby right here will fry a vampire's ass like some chicken" replied Junior as he admired the weapon in his hand.

"That's some fine craftsmanship son. What's gotten you working so hard?"

Junior smiled, "Glad you asked pop. I want to join a guild. I want to be a hunter like you"

Harvey looked at his son like he was crazy, "Absolutely not, look at you"

Junior stood there, looking at his dad. He was not like his father. Even though Harvey was in his mid-sixties, he still had a muscular build. He still carried the muscle from his many years of being a hunter. Junior on the other hand was not muscular or athletic. He was bi-racial, so he was a light skin version of his dark skinned father. Junior only stood 5' 7" with a slender build. What he lacked in muscle, he made up for with his intellect. Graduating with a degree in engineering, he helped his father with the family business of making weapons. Junior knew if he was going to become a hunter he was going to need to find a way to make up for his lack of physical prowess. So, he began experimenting with making weapons that fired ultraviolet rays. Thus, creating his line of Sun weapons. Now that they're completed he was ready to become a hunter.

The only thing left to do was convincing his father to let him become a hunter, and already he is not with the idea.

"What do you mean, look at Me.?"

"I mean look at you son, you're you. You're no Hunter son. You've never seen a werewolf, vampire or a witch in real life"

"Junior stood there in silence. It was true; he hasn't seen any type of supernatural beings. But that didn't change his mind on becoming a hunter.

"Exactly, you wouldn't know what to do standing face to face with one of those creatures"

"You showed me how to defend myself, I'll be fine. I'm old enough to make my own decisions pop. The vampire that almost crippled you, and killed mom is still out there running free. He has to pay for what he did to you and mom!" shouted Junior.

"Is that what all this is about? Junior you have to let that go. I've made my peace with that a long time ago, you should too. Besides that, vampire could be anywhere in the world" replied Harvey.

Junior just ignored his father's request, hell bent on avenging his mother's death. "I understand your concern pop but I'm going to be a hunter whether you like it or not" said Junior sternly.

Harvey continued to try to convince his son how being a hunter was a bad idea, but his cries fell on deaf ears. "Son, I know how you feel, but listen……" Before he could finish his sentence, the sound of the door buzzer interrupted their discussion.

"Saved by the bell" whispered Junior under his breath.

Harvey got up from his seat, making his way upstairs to answer the door. "Looks like we have customers, we will finish this discussion later"

"There is nothing more to discuss pop, my mind is made up" said Junior returning his attention to his invention.

Harvey shuck his head as he limped up the steps back to the pawnshop above. When he opened the employee only door, he is surprised to find a man and a woman. The man had his back towards Harvey as he was taking interest in the antiques. The female he could see, she was looking in one of the glass cases that housed some fine jewelry. She appeared to be in her early twenties, light skin, with long silky black hair that was pulled into a ponytail. He slowly walked over to the counter grabbing his pistol that rested under the register.

Pointing his pistol at the two intruders, "I don't know how you two got in here but we are closed. So unless you want to leave on a stretcher I suggest you leave now!" replied Harvey.

"Is that how you greet an old friend?" replied Alex with a smile as he turned to face Harvey.

Surprised at who stood in his shop, Harvey lowered his gun. "Alexander muthafucking Knight, boy I haven't seen you in ages" replied Harvey as he greeted Alex with a handshake hug.

"Time has definitely been good to you"

"Well you know it's one of the perks that come with immortality. Sorry to barge in like this, but we came to see if you were still in business"

"You plan on getting back in the game? I thought you was done after that last episode you had" said Harvey.

"Let's just say I found new motivation" smiled Alex as his looked in Ravens direction. "Harvey, I would you to meet Raven"

Raven walked over to Alex and Harvey, "It's a pleasure to meet you" Raven said with a smile.

"Raven, this is Harvey. He is very good friend of mine" said Alex

"Pleased to meet you Raven" said Harvey as they shuck hands.

"You have a lovely establishment"

"If you think this is nice, then you're gonna love this. Follow me"

Harvey led them back through the "employees only" door as they made their way downstairs into the workshop below.

"Now this is the real establishment. Junior we have customers"

Raven and Alex were in awe at the sight of Harvey's workshop. It was like stepping into a toyshop for gun lovers. Everything you would ever need was within these four walls.

"I see you haven't lost you touch Harvey, these weapons look amazing"

"I can't take all the credit for this. Junior had his part in this as well"

"Junior?"

"Yeah he has grown up into a fine engineer."

From the back of the shop, emerged Junior with his safety goggles on, "You call me pop?" replied Junior.

"Yes, we have customers. I would like to introduce you to you my old friend Alex and his friend Raven"

Raven waves at Junior as Alex gives him a head nod.

"Son they came to get equipped, why don't you show them what you've been working on."

"Sure, thing pop" replied Junior as he walked over to a nearby wall. He flipped the light switch on the wall causing the wall to come to life. The wall opened up revealing some futuristic looking weapons.

"What are those?" replied Raven with wide eyes.

"These are my pride and joy. It took me a long time to make these" said Junior as he took a sawed-off shotgun off the shelf.

"You have out done yourself with these weapons Junior. Harvey, I know you're very proud" Alex replied.

"Yes sir. He is taking the family business into the future. Son, they're all yours."

Junior smiled. He has been eager to give a demonstration, he has been practicing his pitch for weeks and today was the day.

"All right, lady and gentlemen if I could have your attention. All the weapons you see here can shoot a variety of ammunition from standard rounds, silver rounds and now UV solar rounds. I was able to synthesis ultraviolet light into these shell casings. This right here, I call it the sunburst. It's a modified sawed-off shotgun that shoots off silver buckshot rounds or a concentrated burst of UV light, very good for close quarters"

Junior puts the sawed off back on the wall, then grabs his next weapon. "This right here is my personal favorite. I call it the Sunshot, a sniper's dream come true. This bad boy can shoot a beam of concentrated sunlight. Using these solar panels to gather sunlight it never need runs out of ammo. It can also shoot standard and silver rounds as well. Not to mention the scope has night and heat vision capabilities. For you little lady I have the perfect companion."

He returns the Sunshot back on its display on the wall, as he grabs one of the hand cannons.

"This is ideal for any hunter. Like the others, it can shoot a variety of rounds and it can shoot these explosive UV rounds."

Junior hands Raven the hand cannon. It felt light in her hand; she imagined it would be much heavier, as she aimed down the sight of the gun.

"Son, I'm very impressed" smiled Harvey.

"Harvey, I must admit, your son has skills" said Alex

"Alex, I saved the best for last. You and pops is going to love this" replied Junior with excitement. Sitting underneath the rifle was a sword in a black sheath.

"I made this for those who like to get physical" said Junior as he removed the sword from its sheath. The blade was of normal length, and made of silver, however the center of the blade looked transparent or invisible.

"As you can see the blade is made of silver, while the center of the blade is missing. Now do you see this thin strip of material that runs from the hilt all the way to the tip of the blade?" asked Junior.

Everyone nodded their heads yes, as Junior pressed a small black button located on the hilt of the blade. The thin sliver of material began to glow a neon blue color, as it hummed like a zap light.

"This is a concentrated beam of ultraviolet light that will cut through vampires like a hot knife through butter baby, while still giving the durability of the silver blade making this a worthy companion for any sword bearer."

"Son you have truly outdone yourself this time" replied Harvey full of pride.

"Junior all of these weapons are amazing" said Raven

"I agree little man; I've never seen weapons like these. You might as well take my wallet and give me back how much you think I should have" said Alex.

Harvey and the others laugh.

"Excellent! Raven, go ahead and pick out what you like, and Junior will package it up for you" said Harvey. "I have some business to discuss with Alex"

"Ok, Pop I'll take care of her" said Junior

"Thanks Mr. Harvey…" said Raven with a warm smile.

Harvey leaves Junior to assist Raven with her weapon selection, while he took Alex to his office. The office decorated like a hunter's trophy room with antique and modern weapons lining the walls, several bookshelves with a variety of books, strange artifacts from his many travels and more weapons of course. Harvey offered Alex a seat as he took his seat in his brown leather captain's chair. Alex examined the variety of memorabilia that decorated the office before finally taking a seat in front of Harvey's Mahogany wood desk, Alex grabbed a picture frame off the desk.

"That was a long time ago" said Harvey.

Alex smiled looking at the old photo of him; a younger Harvey and two others.

"Yeah, this was the good old days. So, I know you didn't bring me back her to stroll down memory lane, what's on your mind" said Alex placing the picture frame back in its rightful place on the desk.

"I have a favor to ask" said Harvey.

"I'm listening" replied Alex curiously.

"First thing first, is Raven what think she is?"

"Yeah, that kind of just happened, she was dying and I couldn't let her...."

"But you could have just given her your blood."

Alex didn't say anything, because he knew this was true, but Alex didn't want to just save Raven he wanted more, to give her more.

"You know what, I totally get it. Don't mind me I'm just a nosy old man." smiled Harvey. "The real reason, I brought you back here is because earlier Junior and I got into a little argument. He wants to be a Hunter like his mom and I. He is hell bent on getting revenge for her death."

"Ok, what does any of that have to do with me" asked Alex

"Well it looks like Raven and you are about to join the guild, and I was hoping Junior could go with you"

"Are you crazy!? I have my hands full with her, and this whole Alpha, beta relationship"

"I understand, but I would feel much better if he was out there with someone I can trust. Besides, with all the new weapons you're getting, you are going to need someone to keep up the maintenance on them."

"I don't know man; I don't want to be responsible if something happens to your son"

"He is going to do it whether I like it or not, at least this way I know someone is watching his back. How about this, I'll even throw in some extra fire power free of charge"

"You drive a hard bargain, Ok, I take him with me. But if he gets on my nerves I'll compel his ass back into infancy"

"HAHAHA! Deal, let's go share the good news"

Harvey and Alex exit the office returning to where Junior was showing Raven how to properly care for her new hand cannon.

"Junior how's everything going?" ask Harvey

"Everything is great, just finishing up the weapon handling" replied Junior.

"This gun is awesome, I can't wait to use it" said Raven excitedly.

"Excellent. Son I have something to tell you. After our discussion, earlier I realized you're no longer a little boy, and I can't stop you from doing what you want to do. So as a favor to me Alex has agreed to let you join him and Raven as Hunters"

Filled with joy, Junior shouted like a praise dancer catching the Holy Ghost. "Pop, are you serious?" said Junior

Smiling from ear to ear Harvey replied, "Yes, son. If you are going to be a hunter, you need to be with people you can trust"

"Thanks Pop, thanks Alex, I will not let you guys down"

"This day is getting better and better, new weapons and now our pack is getting bigger" smiled Raven.

"Pack?" asked a confused Junior.

"Oh, I almost forgot to mention one small thing" replied Harvey.

"Well, since Raven let the cat out the bag, would you like to do the honors?" said Alex.

"Oooh was that supposed to be a secret?" replied Raven as she covered her mouth with her hand.

Alex smiled, "It's ok, if he is going to be working with us might as well show him"

Still confused about what everyone was talking about, Junior said, "Is anyone going to tell me what is going on?"

Alex nodded his head to Raven, as Raven replied by shrugging her shoulders. She looked at Junior, closing her eyes, taking a deep breath. When she opened her eyes, they glowed their luminous yellow hue.

Junior watched with wide eyes as his mouth hung open, "Holy shit, you're a werewolf" Junior said softly. Raven smiled as she pointed towards Alex. As Junior made eye contact with Alex, he saw that his eyes too glowed, not yellow like Ravens, but a bright furious ruby red.

"Welcome to the pack" smiled Alex.

Meanwhile

Smoking a cigarette, looking into the evening sky, two security guards stood posted outside of an unmarked building. With no visible windows, and a large steel door that was the only way in or out of the abandoned warehouse. Its location was only known by its prestige clientele, the warehouse sat at the end of a one-way street that opened up into large a parking lot. For an abandoned building in the middle of nowhere, the guards were heavily armed. They were standing guard for one of several facilities like this throughout the city. Due to the Council; which is formed of one member of each group of the supernatural world, one witch, one vampire, one werewolf and a human, they were created to keep peace between the different bodies of the supernatural world. One of the first things they agreed upon was harming humans was forbidden, thus, creating the ban on vampires feeding on humans. Within these walls, vampires come to feed on humans in a safe and discreet manner, away from the seeing eye of the council. This service wasn't cheap; this is more for those who embrace the ways of old; feeding on humans. Tasting the blood straight from the vein is more satisfying than drinking it from a blood bag. The two men have stood guard at this location for several months and not once have they had to use their weapons or even had any issues for that matter.

Every night the high-profile clients pulled up in their luxury vehicles; the local vampires vehicle of choice was a lavish all black SUV. These vehicles have been modified with thick tinted bulletproof glass, heavily armed bodies with reinforced steel frames and a list of secret modifications specific to its owner. Driven by chauffeur, clients are dropped off at the door then escorted into the building by the two men who are standing guard out front. The guards are the only ones who can open the double steel doors. Located next to the door is a biometric scanner that reads the palm print of the two guards. The guard placed his palm on the scanner, opening the heavy door. The steel doors open slowly like a drawbridge of a castle. Waiting on the other side of the door holding an iPad waiting to greet the client is a young female receptionist. The receptionist, dressed in a stunning mini black dress that hugged her slim, runway model frame, would take them to the back of the building where the real fun is.

As the steel doors slowly began to close, sealing the client within the build. A dark figure emerged from the shadows dressed in black tactical body armor. Their identity concealed by a helmet, the unknown assassin charged the two guards. Without hesitation, the guards aimed their assault rifles, firing on the uninvited guest. The armor-clad intruder unsheathed a sword that rested on their back, using it to deflect the oncoming barrage of gunfire.

"Don't let them enter the building "shouted one of the guards as he continued to open fire. The intruder leaped into the evening sky, throwing their sword into the chest of one of the guards. The other guard kept firing until he was out of ammo. He desperately tried to reload his weapon but the intruder was too fast. Before he could insert the clip into his weapon, the intruder snatched their sword with the wolf head hilt from the other guard's chest. The last remaining guard dropped the clip to his rifle, causing his natural survival instincts to kick in, swinging his rifle to deflect the intruder's attempts to cut him, but the blade sliced through the rifle and the guard. With no time to waste the intruder slid through the steel doors just seconds before they sealed themselves shut. The receptionist and the vampire client stood motionless in the center of the room staring at the intruder. The receptionist tried to activate the emergency system from tablet without drawing the attention of the intruder, but to no avail. The intruder reached for the gun that was secured in the holster on their hip. Aiming it at the receptionist and her client, the intruder opened fire. The gun fire echoed throughout the hallway, causing vampires to come out of their private rooms in a panic. The intruder reached in a pouch located on the small of their back, retrieving devices the size of small calculators.

The intruder sprinted down the hallway tossing the electrical devices onto nearby pillars. The devices attached to the pillars beeping to life as a red light blinked and flickered. The intruder made it to the back of the facility as its occupants frantically escaped the building. In the center of the room was a black oak chair that resembled that of a thrown, with its crushed velvet seat and back rest. Sitting in the chair legs crossed, holding a cognac glass filled with blood was a man dressed in black robes. The upper body had a hood with the center shaped to resemble that of an eagle's beak which was connected to the robes, with the torso bearing an open collar and a black-grey fur padding on his right shoulder. The lower part of the robes were double layered, with the back of the robes trailing down to be longer than the front. The man stood up to reveal around his waist a long red sash with pouches attached to the belt. To complete his outfit the man wore a white kabuki mask with no lips and the eyes of the mask shaped like the eyes of an owl. In the center of the mask was a black dot with gold flames around it.

The intruder unsheathed their, sword with the wolf's head on the hilt.

"I've been waiting for you" said the masked man in a robotic voice. He grabbed his sword that was resting against the black oak chair. "Now before you go a blow up this fine establishment, you're going to have to show me you know how to use that weapon of yours.

The intruder didn't say a word, as they charged the masked man. Slashing at the masked man's face, without removing his sword from its sheath, he deflected the intruder's attacks.

"Very good, but you lack focus" replied the masked man.

The intruder didn't stop their assault, as they slashed high then immediately low. The masked man evaded the attacks still not removing his sword from its sheath.

"I'm impressed, but I think that's enough. Don't want to get cut by that vicious blade of yours" said the masked man as he removed his sword from its sheath. The silver blade twinkled under the lights.

"Now let's play" said the masked man.

He leaped over the intruder, flipping in the air as he simultaneously swung his sword, slashing at their head. The intruder was barely able to keep up with the mask mans speed as they deflected the attacks that came from above. He landed on his feet, pressing on his attack. It was like he was attacking the intruder from every angle at once. Unable to keep up, the intruder was hit in the right arm. A female voice screamed in pain from behind the intruder's helmet as she dropped her sword. The masked man finished his attack slashing at the female intruder's leg sending her crashing to the ground.

The intruder was down on one knee as they removed their helmet, revealing their identity. Breathing heavily, Eve threw her helmet on the ground, then grabbed the wound on her right arm.

"Just make it quick" she said as she mentally prepared herself for the inevitable.

The masked man stood in front of Eve wiping the blood from his silver sword before returning it to its sheath on his hip.

"You have been trained very well Eve."

Eve looked at the masked man with a puzzled look, "How do you know my name?"

"I know everyone who wants to join the Order of the Black Sun. Throughout the ages I have been called many names, you may know by my more popular name. They call me the Silver blade, and I must say I am very pleased with your development. This was your final test and you passed with flying colors my dear" said the silver blade in his robotic voice.

"But I couldn't beat you" replied Eve holding her head down in shame. "I am not worthy"

The Silver blade kneeled down, gently placing his hand on Eve's soft brown skin, "My dear I'm over a hundred years older than you. You would never be able to defeat an older vampire head on. But with further training you will be an unstoppable force."

"How can I trust you, I was under the impression someone else was the leader of the Order" Eve replied.

The Silver blade let out laugh that his modified kabuki mask made robotic. "You are a smart young lady" he replied as he stood up. "You have earned my trust, now let me earn yours" The Silver blade removed his hood, revealing his kabuki mask, which was more helmet than a mask. He pressed a button on the side of helmet, as it opened with a hiss. Eve watched as The Silver blade removed his helmet.

"Now do you trust me" said The Silver blade as he unveiled his identity to Eve.

Eve was shocked at who was behind the kabuki mask, "You muthafucka" she replied.

"Wouldn't it been easier just to tell me you were the Silver blade?" she asked.

He sealed his mask once more, concealing it with his hood. "I had to first know if I could trust you, now I do. Now get up and let's finish what you started" replied The Silver blade as he extends his hand to help Eve to her feet.

The Silver blade escorted Eve out of the building, where Dolla was standing next to an all-black Hummer waiting.

"Looks like she passed the final test" said Dolla as he opened the door for the Silver Blade.

"Yes, but there is still one last thing she has to do" replied the Silver blade as he handed Eve a small device that looked like a lighter with a small red button, that was glowing red.

"Would you like to do the honors?" asked the Silver blade. Eve took the detonator and pointed at the large building, "It will be my pleasure" replied Eve as she pressed the red button. The building exploded into a ball of flames. The force from the explosion shock the hummer as debris rained down on the vehicle.

"I, the Silver blade officially welcome you into the Order of the Black Sun" he replied, as the building burned in the background.

UP NEXT.

SEASON FINALE

EPISODE 10

"THE WOODEN DAGGER"

Handcuffed to a stake, sitting in a pile of stones, large pieces of timber and gasoline was a rogue witch by the name of Scarlett Williams. She is wanted for the mass murder of several members of the Trinity Coven. The same coven she denounced months ago after her team mates left her for dead. Scarlett spent the next few months searching for something to aid her in her quest for revenge. After endless days of chasing lead, after lead, she found what she was searching for but not before members of a local hunter's guild; The Wooden Dagger, with the aid of a witch, found her and captured her.

Scarlett is moments away from being burned at the stake. Surrounded by the six remaining members of the Wooden Dagger; each holding a torch in their hand. Standing in front of Scarlet, draped in a black quarter length hooded cloak, New

Orleans native, and right hand to the high priestess of the council, Vaidah LaRue gave her final words to Scarlett.

"Scarlett Williams, you have been found guilty of all chargers. As ordered by the council I hereby sentence you to death by burning at the stake"

Scarlett struggled to get free as she pulled at the chains binding her to the stake.

"So, you guys aren't going to call the Harbingers to collect me?" replied Scarlett.

One of the male hunters; walked up to Scarlett. He looked down on her with murderous intent in his eyes.

"All those innocent people you killed, the hunters that sacrificed their lives to help capture you. The council declared you too dangerous to leave alive"

The other hunters in attendance all shouted in agreement.

"Just set that bitch of fire" shouted a hunter.

"Yeah cook her fucking ass" shouted another"

The cheering from the hunters continued, making Vaidah uncomfortable. Even though Scarlett had done terrible things, as a fellow witch, seeing another burning at the stake was a little barbaric.

"Well I think that is my Que. She maybe evil, but this is a cruel punishment. This is something I'm not interested in being a witness to" replied Vaidah as she walked away from the hunters disappearing into the darkness of the night.

"Suit yourself, more fun for us" smirked the male hunter who stood in front of Scarlett.

The hunters waited to make sure Vaidah was gone, "I thought she would never leave" replied the hunter who stood in front of Scarlett.

He returned his gaze upon her. Without warning, he slapped her in the face with a backhand. Scarlett's head whipped to the right as blood sprayed out her mouth.

"That's for my fallen brethren" replied the hunter. He slaps her again, "And that's for all of us"

The hunters cheered him on as he continued to hit Scarlett, until they were interrupted by the sound of a robotic voice.

"Now that's no way to treat a lady" replied the robotic voice from the shadows.

The hunters turned towards the direction of the voice where two figures, one male and one female emerged from the shadows.

"Who do you think you are? This has nothing to do with you, asshole" replied the hunter

"Yeah, you have picked the wrong woods to take your lady on a romantic walk. Now turn around before we embarrass you in front of her" replied another hunter.

The two-continued approaching the hunters until they were close enough for the hunters to get a good look at them. The hunters didn't recognize the female with her short pixie hairstyle and brown skin, but the person she was with was unmistakable. Everybody in the supernatural community would recognize this person. With his black robes and Kabuki mask partially hidden under his hood.

"Holy shit, it's the Silver Blade" shouted one of the hunters.

Eve and the Silver Blade look at each other, "Well let's make this quick" replied the Silver blade.

Eve gave the Silver Blade a smirk as her eyes turned bright emerald green. She reached into the inside pocket of her leather jacket, pulled out a 9mm and opened fire on the group of hunters.

The hunters reached for their weapons but Eve was too fast for them. The first hunter took two bullets to the chest collapsing to the ground. Eve emptied her clip into the second hunter as he tried to find cover, hitting him in his leg, right arm and his back. The hunter's lifeless body slams into the tree before collapsing to the ground. Eve dropped her gun as she continued her assault on the four remaining hunters. By this time, the other hunters have drawn their weapons and are returning firing at Eve. Rolling into cover, Eve shields herself behind the tree where she killed one of the hunters. She picked up the dead man's gun. She releases the clip from the gun, checking the ammo, before returning it back onto the gun. She leaped from behind the tree as she started firing at the remaining hunters. The hunters don't even try to run for cover. Their anger clouded their judgment. Using her vampire speed, Eve dodged the oncoming gunfire. One by one the hunters began to run out of ammo. Eve charged the first hunter who ran out of bullets as he tried to reload his weapon. She tackled him to the ground. As their bodies slammed onto the ground, she used the momentum to roll on top of the hunter, placing her knee on his stomach then shooting him twice in the chest. With her gun now empty, she grabbed her sword from its sheath on her back. She charges the last two hunters who were also out of ammo. She leaped at the closest one to her. He was able to reload his weapon but he was too late. Eve ran up on him, with one fatal swoop she sliced through him and his gun. The hunter screamed in agony as he fell to the ground holding pieces of his gun in both hands. There was only one hunter left. He had already had his weapon reloaded, aiming it at her. With no time to avoid the gunfire, Eve threw her sword at the hunter like it was a tomahawk. The blade hit the hunter in the shoulder, snatching him off the ground and pinning him to the tree.

Scarlett kept her head down the entire time, while the female vampire was shooting. Once the fighting was done, Scarlett looked up to find all the hunters were laying on the ground dead, only the female and her masked companion were left standing.

"How was that" replied Eve as she patted the dirt off her jeans.

The Silver blade pointed at the man who was pinned to the tree with her sword, "You missed one"

"I just killed five hunters by myself and all you can say is, I missed one?" replied Eve

The Silver Blade made his way over to Scarlett who was completely terrified. He kneeled down to her as she tried desperately to break free.

"Relax, we are not here to hurt you" said the Silver blade trying to sound reassuring, which was a difficult task since his mask made his voice sound electronic. "I'm going to remove these shackles. If you try anything, my lovely assistance here will not hesitate to add you to her growing body count. Do you understand?" asked the Silver blade.

Scarlett nodded her head yes.

"Excellent" replied the Silver blade as he broke Scarlett's shackles with his bare hands.

The Silver Blade stood back to give Scarlett her space. Scarlett stood up, and then walked out of the fire pit. Her gasoline soaked clothes clung to her body accentuating her curves. She was around 5'7" with golden brown skin. Her dark brown hair came down to her shoulders. The hair that covered her right eye had streaks on red.

"So, what does the Silver blade want with a witch like me "asked Scarlett massaging her wrist.

"Oh, so you know who I' am" replied the Silver blade

"Of course, everyone has heard the tales of the Silver blade. So, what are you doing here?"

"Well Eve and I had a little wager going on; I said she wouldn't be able to take out all six hunters by herself. Unfortunately, I was right."

"Technically I did. As you can see he just isn't dead yet" scoffed Eve.

"Which technically means he isn't dead yet, so hand it over" he replied with his hand out.

"Whatever!" said Eve, as she reached into her pants pocket, pulling out a gold coin to give to the Silver blade.

"Thank you!" He replied. "Now that we have that out the way, what is your name?"

"My name is Scarlett Williams"

"Of the Trinity coven?" he asked

"Yes, you've heard of me?" she asked.

"Hahahaha! Told you" shouted Eve

The Silver blade looked back at Eve, then handed her back the gold coin.

"Thank you!" said Eve with a grin

"Yes, I've heard of you. I was told you killed your entire family as well as several members of your coven."

"They tried to deny me what was rightfully mine" said Scarlett in a sinister voice.

"Did you at least get what you were searching for?" He asked.

"Yes, I finally found what they tried to deny me, but before I could use it these idiot hunters found me. I would have got away if it wasn't for that bitch Vaidah. Enough about me, you still haven't told me why you helped me?"

"You see, I'm putting together a team, and I need someone like you on my side. I hate to see someone with such potential go to waste. If you join me, you will be able to dish out some well-deserved revenge among many other benefits"

"Count me in! You don't have to convince me, I just need to handle some unfinished business" replied Scarlett excitedly.

"Excellent! You go ahead and take care of whatever business you need to attend to. I don't need you distracted. Once you are finished give us a call and I'll have someone pick you up and bring you to us" said the Silver Blade as he handed her a Matte black business card with only a shiny telephone number on it. "Now Scarlett, if you betray me I assure you, you will wish they set your pretty ass on fire"

"I hear you loud and clear" replied Scarlett.

"That's great and all, but what are we going to do about him" said Eve interrupting their conversation.

They all turn to look at the hunter still alive pinned to the tree by Eve's sword.

The Silver blade walked over to the hunter. "I have something special planned for him" said the Silver blade, as he pulled Eve's sword out of the hunter's shoulder.

Back at Alex's mansion that sat on a deserted island just off the Amalfi Coast, Raven, and Alex sat in the living room, while Junior was still freaking out about the method used to get them to the island. He took himself on a tour of the home, marveling at its beautiful Victorian architecture. He could tell most of the furniture, portraits and other artifacts in the castle were older than him.

"Alex this place is amazing" shouted Junior as he returned to the living room.

Raven sat on the couch examining her new weapons that Alex purchased for her as a gift for completing her training, Alex stood next to the fireplace holding a cognac glass filled with a cognac and blood infused liquid.

"So, let me get this straight, you are both vampire and werewolf?" asked Junior as he took a seat in a chair that looked like a miniature throne with its exquisite details in the wood and crushed velvet padding on the seat and backrest.

"That's right" replied Alex, taking a sip of his drink.

"That explains why you look the same in that photo on pops desk of ya'll when he was a young hunter" said Junior as he puts the pieces together in his head.

"I know it's a lot to process right now Junior, but we have work to do. Since you two want to be hunters, I'm going to have you guys join the Wooden Dagger guild."

"That's the same guild you and pops were members of, right?" said Junior

"Right"

"Oh, this is going to be so exciting!" smiled Raven

"This way you guys can get some hands on experience, learn how to work together as a team, and gather some Intel so you can find your friend Eve."

"Why does it sound like you're not coming with us?" asked Raven crossing her arms

"Wait, you're not coming with us Alex?" replied Junior.

Alex takes another sip of his drink, "Oh I won't be able to do that! The guild master will recognize my face, and it will be pretty hard to explain why I haven't aged. Besides I have some person business to attend to. You and Junior will join the guild gather info and if you hear anything about Jag and his crew let me know" said Alex.

"Who?" asked Junior still confused about what was going on.

"It's a long story, I'll have to tell you about later" said Raven.

"Raven, there is one more thing I need to tell you. Out there you may encounter other wolvers. They will try to test you because you're not in a pack, they don't take kindly to Omegas"

"What the hell is an Omega? You two better start talking English around here!" said Junior

"It's a werewolf that doesn't have a pack" replied Raven

"But you two are a pack though?"

"Yes, but my existence is currently unknown, and I would like to keep it that way so my enemy doesn't realize he didn't finish the job, so keep your mouth shut Junior!"

"Hey man, I ain't gonna say shit!" said Junior as he pretended to zip his lips shut.

"That's what I wanted to hear, because they will test you two out there. Just make sure you politely kick they ass. After all, you are representing the Knight pack.

"This is so exciting! I'm finally going to be a hunter, and track down my mother's killer" said Junior.

"About that" said Alex placing his drink on a nearby table next to Raven. He walked over to Junior who was still seated.

"I don't mind you looking into your mother's murder, just be prepared to deal with what you find"

Junior stood up from his seat, "I have to do this. It's the only thing that keeps me going, the only reason I built these weapons and wanted to join the guild. I'll find my mother's killer and make him pay for what he has done to me and pops."

Alex places his hand on Juniors shoulder, "I'm just making sure you're ready, you might not like what you find out if you go down this path."

"Don't worry; I'll help you find your mother's killer. A vampire killed my best friend right in front of me, so I know how you feel" said Raven as she made her way over to where Alex and Junior were standing.

"Thanks, I'll help you find your best friend's killer too" replied Junior.

"Well that's great, if you two are done with the sentimental stuff, we should get going. The sun is starting to set. We need to get back to the city before dark" said Alex.

THE WOODEN DAGGER

Hidden in plain sight in the downtown area was the Wooden Dagger; home and name of the hunter's guild of the city. The exterior looks like an abandoned building with no visible sign to identify you are at the right place. If you weren't paying attention you wouldn't even notice it was even there. At one point many years ago, the Wooden Daggers was a big deal in the supernatural community. Some of the finest hunters were members of this guild. Hunters from near and fear would flock here to be members of this guild; the Wooden Dagger. But today it is nothing but a shadow of its former self. After an unfortunate chain of events that happened to the Guild master, hunters left the guild in seek of a more honorable leader.

Now the guild only has a handful of loyal members, and on this night, they're on a bounty to capture a rogue witch by the name of Scarlett Williams. Standing at a large board, the size of the entire wall filled with pictures of bounties; Deuce and her brother Tre' searched for their next job. Deuce was a tall, light skin African American woman with an athletic build. Her long black hair swayed back and forth as she glanced over the hundreds of wanted posters that plastered the bounty board.

"We have been doing this for a while now and we still haven't got any closer to finding him. It's like he just disappeared. How we gonna avenge our pack if we can't find one damn wolf?" replied Tre' as he leaned against the wall next to the wanted board.

Tre' was the younger brother of Deuce. He was a little shorter than his sister, with a slightly darker brown complexion with his hair in long dreads. What he lacked in speed he made up with pure strength. Together they made a good team, what the other lacked, the other picked up the slack.

Deuce never looked away from the board, "We will find him soon, and when we do I'm gonna shove my gun down his throat. I just hope he hasn't started his own pack. That will cause us more problems" she said as she continued her search.

"Fuck that! If he has a pack that's gonna make him damn near invincible for a pair of Omega's, unless we find us our own pack"

"Good thing we have the guild. If it wasn't for the Guild Master taking us in, one of those other packs would have surely tried to take us out." replied Deuce.

"But now that we are hunters, nobody is going to let us join their pack. Ugh, I miss being in a pack" said Tre' as he rested his head on the wall, staring at the ceiling.

"That's fine, because once I kill him; I'll be able to rebuild our pack. Until then, the Wooden Dagger is our pack" said Deuce.

Tre' looked around the empty bar. The only people in the bar besides his sister and himself were the three-old man playing cards in the back of the building, and the bartender who was currently sleeping at the bar. "Yeah, some pack, and those guys in the back aren't even hunters"

"Don't worry little brother; we will be back in a pack, you'll see" replied Deuce, looking back at her brother with a smile. She returned her attention back to the board of bounties. Tre' took a seat at a nearby table as his indecisive sister found them a bounty that paid well, but doesn't get them killed. Just as Deuce is finally making her selection, her train of thought is interrupted by the sound of someone entering the bar. Deuce and Tre' both whipped their heads towards the door to see who had found their way into the Wooden Dagger. They thought it was the others coming back from completing their bounty; instead two unfamiliar faces were making their way to the bar. It was a male and female. Both looked a little too young to be in a bar.

The male wore glasses, light skin, tall and lanky. He was dressed like a hunter but he didn't look like a hunter. He looked more like he should be working for tech support at some electronics company. The female was also of light complexion. She was much shorter than the male, with long, silky raven black hair that she had up in a ponytail. She too was dressed like a hunter, but didn't appear to be the type to get her hands dirty. Deuce and Tre' watched as their new guest strolled up to the bar as they both noticed a familiar scent.

Standing at the bar, Junior slapped his hand on the bar counter as he looks around for some service. "What's a brother gotta do to get some service around here?" he shouted

Sitting at the end of the bar with his head down in a drunken slumber was an unshaven Caucasian male who looked like he was in his early thirties. The banging on the counter made him jump out his seat as he stumbled to his feet. "Alright, alright, hold your fucking horses" barked the man slurring his words. He made his way behind the counter, walking like a zombie moaning and groaning as he finally made it to wear Junior and Raven stood.

"Excuse my friend, he doesn't get out much. We are looking for the Guild Master" replied Raven

Now that the man was standing in front of them, they could get a better look. His dusty blonde hair was cut low. He had two claw marks over his left eye that was covered by a black leather eye patch. He reached under the bar to grab a bottle of brown liquid to pour himself a drink.

"Why you looking for him? He doesn't owe you any money does he" he replied as he leaned in like he was trying to keep a secret.

Raven stepped back as she covered her nose. The man reeked of alcohol as if he had been swimming in pool of it.

"No sir. Me and my friend here want to join this Guild" said Raven, slightly disgusted with the man behind the bar.

"Yeah, we want to be hunters" said Junior.

The man behind the bar tried to focus his good eye on Raven and Junior. "The two of you's?? Want to be hunters?" he asked as he busted out laughing. He took a shot of the brown liquid, and poured himself another shot. He glanced at Junior, then leaned in close to get a better look, as if he seen his face before.

"I knew you look familiar, you Harvey's boy! Boooooy you ain't nothing but a light skin version of your daddy! Wait, does your daddy know you here?"

"Yes, he knows I'm here. How do you know my old man" asked Junior as his cheeks became flushed from embarrassment?

"I should call him. I don't need him limping his old ass in here trying to start shit"

Raven beings to get annoyed with the man behind the bar as he continues his conversation with Junior. Finally fed up she slammed her hand on the wooden bar counter, "Is the Guild Master here or not?" barked Raven.

"Little girl you are looking at him!" replied the man behind the bar.

Raven and Junior look at each other unable to believe that this drunken fool was the Guild Master of the Wooden Dagger.

"You're the Guild Master?" asked Raven.

Still in shock, as he realized that he was in the presents of his childhood hero, besides his father. Junior replied, "You're Jacob Martin? Thee Jacob Martin, but you're so, young?"

"Yep, it's me, in all my glory" smirked Jacob.

Without warning Jacob collapsed, knocking his drink over as he crashed to the floor. Watching from the bounty board, Deuce and Tre' saw their leader fall behind the bar. They rush over to the bar, to aid Jacob. Deuce leaps over the bar, while Tre' runs around to the other side. As the two hunters help Jacob to his feet, Raven starts to pick up on a strange scent. It was familiar, yet it was different. She hasn't smelled this particular scent since she left Japan. If finally dawned on her what scent she was picking up on. These two hunters were werewolves.

Raven's eyes, now glowing their luminous yellow hue, she was excited to finally meet other wolves in the city. She blurt out, "You guys are werewolves!"

The words caught Deuce and Tre' off guard causing Tre' to let go off Jacob as his unconscious body crashed back to the floor.

"I knew one of you were werewolf!" shouted Tre"

"Fool, help me with the Guild Master" shouted Deuce as she struggled to get Jacob off the floor.

"Oh, my bad sis" replied Tre' as he assisted with getting Jacob to his feet.

They carried the Guild Master to the closest table, as Raven followed behind them, Junior stayed seated at the bar. Deuce propped the Guild Master up in the chair. Still passed out, he just slumps over banging his head on the table with a loud thud.

"Well I guess I'll pour my own drink" Junior said to himself as he made himself a drink before joining the others. Deuce, Tre' and Raven sat at the table as the Guild Master laid his head on the table, still in his drunken slumber. There was an awkward silence at the table. There hasn't been a new werewolf in the city in a very long time. The Alpha that led the wolves in this city was also a member of the Council, so it was very unlikely he was inducting new betas into his already large pack. So where did this werewolf come from? That was the question on Deuce and Tre's mind. Could she be a product of the man they're looking for? Could she lead them to his whereabouts so they can have their revenge? Their minds were filled with hundreds of questions until their train of thought was interrupted by the sound of Junior pulling up a chair to the table, slamming his drink on the table.

"Alright, all this staring is getting creepy. You are all werewolves, so whatever questions you all have let's get it over with and move on" said Junior as he sat down in his wobbly chair.

Tre' looked at Deuce to see if it was okay to speak. Deuce gave him the ok by slightly nodding her head yes.

"Ok, what's your name?" asked Tre'

"My name is Raven and this is my loud mouth partner in crime Junior" replied Raven.

"Were you born a werewolf? Where is the rest of your pack?" he asked

"No, I wasn't born a werewolf; I was bitten over a year ago...."

"Bitten?" said Deuce, interrupting Raven. "You telling us you were bitten? Did you know who bite you?"

With a confused look on her face, Raven struggled to remember. She could see his face in her mind but was unable to remember who he was.

"I, I don't know. All I can remember is I was at this party, someone shot me and I thought I was dead, but then I woke up the next morning on my couch. I started to notice I wasn't the same anymore" replied Raven, still unsure why she couldn't remember.

Deuce and Tre' look at each other as they both find her story hard to believe. "So, you're an Omega like us? We are without a pack too" said Tre'

"Our Alpha was murdered right in front of us by a member of our own pack. He tried to kill us too, but we survived" said Deuce. Raven could see the hurt in her eyes as the memories of the incident flooded her mind.

"Yeah, the Guild Master took us in, and we have been members of the Wooden Dagger ever since in search of the man who tried to kill us and wiped out our entire pack. Wait! I have a great idea! Since you guys want to join the Guild, why don't the four of us team up together?"

Deuce didn't like this idea not one bit. She gave her brother a look that would send chills down the spin of the devil himself.

"What? It's a good idea. She is an Omega like us and you know how those wolves treat those without a pack" replied Tre'.

"Oh, we don't want to intrude" replied Raven. She could feel Deuce wasn't fawn of the idea.

"It's not that. It's just we have our own agenda. I wouldn't want to drag you into our problems" said Deuce.

"Like your brother said, we Omega's have to stick together. We would be helping each other" smiled Raven

Deuce leaned back into her chair as she pondered on the possibility of working with this mysterious girl and her friend. Her instincts tell her that these two were no threat to them, but something about Raven's story seem sketchy at best, but the pros outweighed the cons she thought to herself. Besides having these two on their side would mean they could tackle larger bounties, plus Tre' is giving her that puppy dog face.

"Fine, we can work together, but if you slow us down, we will have to cut you off" said Deuce in s stern tone.

"Don't worry about that, we can handle ourselves" replied Raven

"Yes!" shouted Tre' "This is going to be so awesome! Our own little pack!"

"Now that I can drink to" replied Junior as he reached for his drink. He raised his glass as if he was making a toast, when from the front of the bar someone busted into the building stumbling, barely able to stand. Deuce and Tre' recognize the man; he was one of the members of the guild who was supposed to on a bounty. The two rushed over to aid their fellow guild member who was badly injured. As they approached the man, he had his hand over a wound in his shoulder that looked like he was stabbed with a sword. The man had his back up against the wall as he tried to keep himself up on his feet. Deuce and Tre' were just a few feet away from the injured man when he reached into his jacket pulling out his gun. Unaware who the man was, Junior and Raven drew their guns in response.

"Whoa, whoa, whoa! Everybody calm down" shouted Deuce as she put her hands in the air

"Gus, what happened to you? Where is everyone else?" asked Tre', who had his hands in the air.

"Don't come near me! Everyone is dead, they're all dead!" shouted Gus. Tears fell down his face as he pointed his gun at Deuce and the others.

"Raven, Junior, put your guns down, it's ok he is one of us"

"He ain't acting like it" replied Junior, with his gun still pointed at the bleeding hunter.

Deuce slowly started walking towards him. With her hands still in the air, she spoke to him in a calm voice, "Calm down Gus, what do you mean everyone is dead? Who did this to you?"

As the words left Deuces lips, it was like it triggered something inside of Gus. He stopped crying and became still like a zombie or some type of puppet. He was no longer acting frantic or even panicking. He just stood there calm, freakishly calm. He went from pointing the gun at his colleges to pointing the gun at his head.

"This is a message from The Order of the Black Sun. No one is safe from us" said Gus in a monotone voice.

Everyone looked at each other more confused than they were before.

"The Order of what" replied Raven

"Wait, Gus don't………" shouted Deuce.

Before she could finish her sentence, Gus shot himself in the head. The sound echoed through the empty bar as his blood splattered on the wall behind him. The three-old man that sat in the back of the bar playing cards had ducked under their table. The sound even jolted Jacob from his drunken slumber. He looked around as If he forgot where he was as he tried to focus his one good eye.

"What the hell is going on……?." He finally saw what the commotion was about. The horrible sight of one of his own lying on the floor of his guild dead…

2 BE CONTINUED......